I0546223

How Algebra Rejoined the Broken Pieces

Nina Olsson

Grosvenor House
Publishing Limited

This book is published by
Grosvenor House Publishing Ltd
Link House
140 The Broadway, Tolworth, Surrey, KT6 7HT.
www.grosvenorhousepublishing.co.uk

ISBN 978-1-80381-673-9

Dedication

To

you Family

around and

circle all

xxx

loving those

a who

make

Contents

Dedication...iii

Rider...vii

Images/Drawings..ix

Prologue..xi

Part One – New York, Work and Play

Chapter One   Questions 3
Chapter Two   News...8
Chapter Three   Letters..12
Chapter Four   Words and Secrets.............................16
Chapter Five   Thoughts about the War 20
Chapter Six   Feeling Homesick 26
Chapter Seven   Our Night Out 31
Chapter Eight   Cinderella Ballroom.......................37
Chapter Nine   Visit to Cambridge 42
Chapter Ten   Thanksgiving Parade 46

Part Two – Secrets from the Past

Chapter Eleven   Visitors 55
Chapter Twelve   A Surprise Encounter 61
Chapter Thirteen   News from Colorado 65

Chapter Fourteen   Family Ties 69

Chapter Fifteen   Wedding Plans 74

Chapter Sixteen   Telegrams.......................................79

Chapter Seventeen   The Wedding..............................83

Chapter Eighteen   Trouble in Cambridge.................91

Chapter Nineteen   Family Conferences.....................96

Chapter Twenty   Jake 101

Part Three – Rejoining of the Broken Pieces

Chapter Twenty-one   Parting of the Ways..............109

Chapter Twenty-two   Confessions 114

Chapter Twenty-three   So Conflicted 118

Chapter Twenty-four   Burglary...............................123

Chapter Twenty-five   Shipmates 128

Chapter Twenty-six   Warnings...............................134

Chapter Twenty-seven   Circle complete 142

List of Characters and Locations 146

Acknowledgements 151

Research..152

Rider

This is a work of fiction.

Some references are to real people (Babe Ruth of the New York Yankees) and situations of the time.

All other characters, referenced persons, alive or deceased, are purely coincidental.

Images/Drawings

1. BOI Badge — 7
2. Fashion Show — 11
3. Flapper Dress — 21
4. 4 Flappers — 25
5. Roseland Ballroom — 34
6. Bix Biederbecke Orchestra — 39
7. Dancers — 40
8. Thanksgiving Parade (1) — 51
9. Thanksgiving Parade (2) — 51
10. Snow blizzard — 56
11. Astor Hotel — 60
12. Wedding Portrait — 86
13. Boathouse — 86
14. Woodland/Boathouse — 87
15. Wedding Tables — 88
16. New York Yankees — 103
17. Boulder Dam — 133
18. Pier 97 — 139

Prologue

My real name is Anastasia, but, until my early 20s, my travelling name was Anna and my secret name was Algebra. Sounds complicated – well, yes.

After being abandoned by my parents at the age of three, I spent the next 20 years searching for them, with the aid of a number of people. Most notably was my aunt, Ekaterina, known as Katya, or, to me, simply as Aunty K. She travelled with me through various countries, time zones and notable periods of recent history.

Other aunts also helped, Aunt Aninya, with whom I lived for my first 15 years. A simple but happy childhood next to a large lake in Siberia. Also with Aunty Elena, in a cave-like dwelling in Moscow; a very strange two-year existence. Other people helped along the way and for most of the time, I was unaware as to why.

I can't say it was an unhappy life because most of it was a joyful time spent with people that I loved and admired. There were times, however, that I fell into a deep melancholia, unsure of where I fitted into everything, what had happened in the past, and in whom I could trust. Every time I felt settled, I had to move on, leaving behind the few friends I had made.

The one bright light in my life was Aunty K, with whom I lived for several years in Romania. She became my guide and travelling companion in my quest to find answers.

We experienced many things, including being volunteer nurses in Russia during the most appalling war the world had seen, and which had involved many nations. A most traumatic time that had opened my eyes to man's inhumanity to his fellow man, greed, anger and cruelty. There was suffering on a scale not previously seen or experienced. However, all was not completely without hope, as there had been many acts of bravery and selflessness, and the support and friendship of strangers.

My search had led me to America, where I now lived, having found my parents, and settled into life in Jazz Age New York. Here, in this environment, I felt much more at ease. I had a new circle of wonderful friends, all co-workers from my employment at Macy's department store. But, still, I had nagging doubts as to whether I had done the right thing in tracking them down. They, after all, must have had very good reasons to disappear from our homeland of Russia.

This was brought to the fore one evening when there was a knock at my door of my New York haven, and standing there was a strange man, whom I thought I had last seen on the ship that had carried me to America. Holding up a badge, he said, "Miss Neilsson, I must ask you to accompany me..."

Part One
New York,
Work and Play

Chapter One

Questions

As we stepped out into the street, I felt a chill run through my body. I could hear Aunty K's voice in my head telling me to be calm, careful and as confident as possible. Very difficult under the circumstances, but I was determined to do my best.

I turned and smiled at the man, but was met with a stony response. A car was waiting at the kerbside in which were sitting two men – the driver and a young man. I hardly dared to look at them as the reason for this journey had still not been made clear to me. The strange man and I got into the back of the car and we drove off at some speed. I was very afraid, I had heard of things like this happening in Russia but not in America, or so I believed.

We drove through the city, but I couldn't really see where, as the windows appeared to have a tint on them which obscured the view. We finally came to a stop. The door was opened and I could see we were in front of a nondescript brown building that actually looked quite pleasant. I had expected it to look like the one that Aunty Elena had taken me to in Moscow, with the heavy, ominous feeling about it.

The young man allowed himself a hint of a smile as he helped me out of the vehicle. Even though it was early evening, the building had many people going about their business in the brightly lit corridors. I was taken up to the sixth floor, to an office, where inside were three other people. Two women of about my age, secretaries I supposed, and an older man, who made it very clear he was in charge, he had a very officious manner about him. The whole scenario very much reminded me of the time Aunty E. had taken me to that sombre building, and I remembered how uncomfortable I had been.

"Miss Neilsson," he began, "we would like to ask you some questions."

Trying to keep my voice from shaking, I replied that I would be happy to answer what I could, but to please forgive me as my English was limited, mostly for what I needed to know for work purposes.

He smiled, saying, not unkindly, "We will keep this as simple as possible. I wish to know why and how you came to be in America."

I felt a little relieved as this was a story that had been well practised, leaving out some of the details, of course. I started by saying that I was orphaned at age three, and had lived with an aunt who had settled in Romania, where her husband was from, after a life spent with a travelling fair. Sadly, he had since died. On our way back to be with our Swedish relatives, we had become involved in the war and taken off to be nurses, firstly in Russia and then Finland.

4

I became very upset and agitated at my recollections of that terrible time. When we had finally reached Sweden, the decision was taken to travel on to America. My aunt had remarried in Sweden, but I wanted to start a completely new life.

I had heard that New York was the place to be and, through my work at the shipping office in Gothenburg, I was able to book passage, with a fellow worker, who had relatives in Chicago. I had now been in the city for almost two years.

No one said a word and I became increasingly nervous. "Is there a problem?" I asked, sounding much more confident than I felt.

"No, just a slight discrepancy with your papers, about your age."

"My age? I am almost 22."

I had to remember that my papers stated that I was almost three years younger than I actually was, a misconception on Carl Gustav's behalf. Aunty K and I had left it that way to muddy the trail when leaving Sweden.

There was a nodding of heads, and the room had suddenly become very full with the young man and the strange man in there too. It felt very much like an interrogation, though conducted in soft tones. Abruptly, the older man said, "You can go for now, one of our cars will take you home."

The young man told me to follow him down to the car pool, then he, the driver and a very shaken me were driven back to my little apartment.

On reaching my building, the young man let me out of the vehicle, smiled at me, spoke, then he and the car were gone. I stood out on the sidewalk, not knowing what to think. It was quite some time before I gathered my thoughts and went inside.

Home in my safe haven, I burst into tears and all of my anxieties flooded back. They had not asked me anything about my visits to Cambridge – perhaps they didn't know, although I very much doubted that. I went through my answers again and again, to see if I had made any silly mistakes that might jeopardise my story.

I worried too about the parting words of the young man as he got back into the car. "See you again soon," he said very softly. And yet they had an ominous sound to them. I had a very fretful, restless night but, come the morning, back in my normal work routine, I began to relax.

I found out later they were from the Bureau of Investigation (BOI).

Chapter Two

News

I didn't mention what had happened to my friends as I wished to forget the whole experience.

The Bureau of Investigation, had been originally set up in 1908 by Attorney General Bonaparte, on instructions of President Theodore Roosevelt. It consisted of special agents tasked with state security. I couldn't imagine that I posed a threat to the country, but yet there must have been something that had alerted them to my presence.

Work carried on as usual, the store becoming more and more busy. I was still serving on the jewellery counter – a section where I really enjoyed working. My two colleagues, Betty and Emily, were very friendly and helpful, and so my days were spent happily doing something that I liked. I learned that Emily was to leave in the next few months as she was going to live near her daughter who had moved to Buffalo. Her new job was to be childminding her two grandchildren. Life never stood still, with circumstances ever-changing.

The wealth displayed by some of the customers was staggering, but I was not jealous, I had had experiences in my life that were priceless.

8

I thought about Aunty K on many occasions and looked forward to the heart-warming letters that I received from her. Her letters, though infrequent, were full of news of her new life with my now new uncle, Carl. His wealth had made life comfortable for her, for which I was very glad, and it was very evident that they adored each other. A large part of me wanted to be there too.

However, I was not unhappy; our little 'gang' still enjoyed our outings, both afternoons and evenings. The Jazz Age, as it was known, was in full swing, and we enjoyed it as much as everyone else. We worked very hard, and we partied hard. Although America had not suffered the same hardships as Europe during the war, the feeling of living for the moment, following the aftermath of those times, was very prevalent.

I still met up with my mother when I could, but we were very careful to make it appear as random as possible. My visits to my father in Cambridge were curtailed for the present. My visit to the Bureau had worried us all.

Any news from other people, like Aunty E, was achieved by a rather convoluted route, culminating in a letter from Aunty K. It reminded me of the fair network set up many years before, safeguarding my parents.

I liked New York and all that it had to offer, but I felt very homesick on many occasions. I didn't know what I missed more, Russia, Romania or being in Sweden with Aunty K.

One of the letters brought news that Aunt Aninya had died, so that part of my life was truly over. I felt very sad as I had not really appreciated all that she had done for me in those early years. She had treated me like a daughter, cared for me, told me her wonderful stories. I held my little animal bracelet and cried for her and my life that had passed. I thought about the lake people, especially Tomas, my first true friend, and wondered how they were faring in the new Russia under the leadership of Comrade Lenin. Not much news filtered through, but what did spoke of a Russia in turmoil.

My thoughts also turned to Hans, of whom I thought of more and more lately. Very little was known of Romania, and I knew enough not to ask. I hoped he had survived the war years; many people of German descent had suffered purely by association, many being imprisoned.

One day, during our lunch break, Alice asked me what was wrong. "I am so worried about you," she said. "The light seems to have gone out of your eyes."

"Just tired, I guess," I said, "and missing my Aunty Katya."

She nodded and seemed satisfied with my answer. "Hmm, we must go out somewhere special, all of our gang."

"Yes, I would like that," I said with as much enthusiasm as I could muster. Hopefully it would lift my spirits.

A date was decided, and we girls, Alice, Lizzie, Mary and I, decided we should treat ourselves to new dresses to mark the occasion. So, with much excitement, we paid a visit to the clothing department. We had been to some of the lunchtime fashion shows, and although we could not afford the top-of-the-range dresses, we thought there would be something to suit each of us. Besides, it was the department where Mary worked.

Chapter Three

Letters

On my quiet evenings, which, at present, was most of them, I would sit and write letters. We had planned our great night out for the following month, so that was something to look forward to; especially as we all had our new 'flapper' dresses.

Firstly, I would write a short letter to Hannah in Chicago. She had been my travelling companion from Sweden on the SS *Drottningholm* and we had promised to keep in touch. I enjoyed hearing about her life and her family, so very different to what I was experiencing but, for all of that, I was glad I had chosen to stay in New York.

My letters to Aunty K and Carl were very different. There were many hidden messages in them so they had to be composed carefully. I still felt that I was under surveillance, being followed everywhere. Probably my imagination, but my interrogation experience still gave me the occasional nightmare.

Through the letters I would live again the happy times we had while travelling, and the good people we met, and that would inevitably lead me on to Hans. I often wondered what had happened to him after we – Aunty K and I – had left him at Odessa. Was he still in Romania? Did he go home to Suceava? Had he been caught up in the dreadful war? Had he even survived? If so, had he married? Selfishly, I hoped not. I had come to realise that I loved him, and even the great distance between us could not alter that fact.

Those memories would also bring to mind Hercules, the big, gentle horse who had been my transport and friend during our travelling days. He had taught me not to be afraid of horses and life on the road, his gentle breathing being of comfort and making me feel safe.

It had been a strange few years, and although I enjoyed New York, I never truly felt that I was home. I so missed my life with Aunty K, and even Russia. I felt very confused.

My relationship with my parents had not changed; I suppose the long intervening years had made the repairing of our bond very difficult. Not being able to spend much time with them, for various reasons, did not help matters. I was still very wary about arranging any visits as my interview with the sinister little man had left me really shaken. I was still not clear as to what he really wanted, and I was afraid to ask too many questions.

My fondest memories were of Aunty K, who to me had become not only a travelling companion, but a sister, an aunt and, in many ways, a mother.

I had told my mother about the visit to the Bureau so we decided to stop our meetings for a while until we both felt that it was safe. My father hadn't ever come to New York and so it had been several months since I had seen him.

My life felt as if it had lost its purpose, and my longing to go home had grown. But where was home? Aunty K and Carl were in Sweden, Hans in Romania, as far as I knew, and the only ones in Russia were Aunty Elena and Uncle Mikhail, and perhaps some of the lake folk.

Much as I liked my life in New York, in my heart I felt a big hole that could only be filled by going home. I put my pen down for the evening and decided to listen to some music on my newly acquired radio. That would cheer me up, at least for the present. I would write some more tomorrow when, hopefully, I would be in a happier frame of mind.

My work was going well, the store certainly looked after their employees, making us feel as if we were part of a large family. Sales in the jewellery department had increased as life had settled down in the aftermath of the war. Some years had passed and a degree of normality had returned.

There had been a great number of weddings in the past three years, with returning soldiers marrying their sweethearts. Our department had never been busier. I felt quite envious but also happy for them that their love had survived all the dreadful obstacles that had been thrown at them.

It brought flooding back the memories from when I was a Red Cross nurse tending injured Russian and Finnish soldiers from the Eastern Front. Those poor boys, some never to see home again. Of course, I did not speak of any of these things; I just kept them locked in my heart.

The two ladies I worked with, Betty and Emily, noticed a change in me, so, making light of it, I told them I was homesick and they naturally assumed that I meant Sweden.

Chapter Four

Words and Secrets

Our little gang – that is, the people that I first met when coming to work at Macy's store – still had our outings together. These were my first friends; Alice, Lizzie, Mary and the two young men, William and Robert.

Mary and Robert had announced that they were walking out together and so had become our first couple. William and I were still friends but our previous closeness had gone. We were not right for each other, especially as I realised that my heart belonged to Hans. The other two girls were wild young things, wanting to savour all of New York's pleasures. And why not – we were all still young, and they had never suffered the traumatic effects of war and I certainly was not going to enlighten them.

Back in my room at night, I would continue writing my letters. Only the most positive ones would be posted, the others I would keep locked away in a beautiful wooden box with an inlaid marquetry top that my friends had bought for me on my birthday.

It would take many months to receive letters from anyone, so when they came, I would read and re-read them many times, savouring every line. Most of the letters came from Aunty K, as correspondence with Russia was not only very difficult, but frowned upon. Also I didn't know how close of a check was being kept on me by the sinister little man and his colleagues.

Aunty K and I had devised a simple code when sending news, so that only she and I would know of whom she was speaking. Whilst I was enjoying myself in New York, and all the freedom that afforded me, life in Mother Russia was far different.

Following the outcome of the war, now referred to as the Great War, Russia had endured a period of civil war as the various factions had fought for supremacy. Lenin and his party of Bolsheviks had won out and were in charge of all areas of people's lives. A new all-encompassing plan had been put into place, which allowed the people limited privileges and freedoms, but there was still ongoing fighting within the political parties. The feelings of uncertainty for everyone must have been dreadful.

I was so glad that I was away from all of that, but I still worried for Aunty E and her husband, living as they did in the centre of it all, in Moscow. My friend, Tomas, and the lake people – if they had survived the wars – I hoped would be less affected, being so far away in Siberia. However, in this I was wrong. The long arms of the 'Party' stretched everywhere.

Aunty K had also written to her friend, Maria, regarding her house in Romania. At present, Maria's daughter was living there as a temporary onsite caretaker. A good arrangement as Aunty K did not know when she would be able to return to Brasov. She had also written to Valentina, one of the fair folk in Sighisaora, and after many months had received a reply.

The fair network was still in force, and through that, news of Hans and his family had been learnt. He was again in Suceava and had managed to get back his old job, with the shipping company. He was, after all, a very skilled and experienced clerk, with knowledge of several languages and wide-ranging shipping experience. His association with Aunty K and me had long since been forgotten, supplanted by the horrors of the war.

At the end of the letters chain was me, in New York, so you can imagine my surprise and delight to learn that Hans had thoughts of travelling to Sweden, and perhaps on to America. Carl Gustav had agreed to sponsor him and help with any necessary papers.

Details of anyone other than Aunty K, Uncle Carl, and their life in Sweden, was buried within the text of the letters. Whilst we were travelling, prior to my arrival in New York, Aunty K and I had devised a way of passing on information that was private. This was proving to be very useful now, as our lives still had their complications.

My mother had also told me of a game the three sisters used to play whilst growing up around the lake. They had been known as the three little mermaids, and so had used their knowledge of the lake, its contents and surrounds to invent special play words. Aunty K had taught many of these to me, and these were what we used for the secret information.

Aunty K wrote to me in Swedish, but in a simplified form, as English was becoming my major language. My Romanian and Russian were all but forgotten.

The time for our big outing was approaching and we has decided to go to one of the new jazz clubs. New bands, new music and new dances; we were all so excited. Mary and Robert had planned it, saying it would raise our spirits before the winter came again.

Chapter Five

Thoughts about the War

Time has a strange way of passing – quickly when you don't want it to, and very slowly when you do, especially when you are looking forward to something.

Our night out seemed to be taking so long, like other events in my life that always seemed just out of reach. We had chosen our dresses and were working what extra hours we could to pay for them. Mary was keeping them safe for us for any alterations in her department storeroom. Mine was a soft blue, which, according to my friends, perfectly matched my eyes.

I was so excited about the dress; I don't think I had ever owned anything so beautiful. It had a rounded neckline, no sleeves, a dropped waistline, and an uneven hem, like the waves on the sea. It reached to about two inches below my knees. The foundation shift was in blue silk, and the overdress was pale blue tulle with tiny pink rosebuds throughout. On the right, near the shoulder, was attached a large pink rose. I absolutely loved it. I did my best to draw it into my next letter to show Aunty K.

My hair was cut short, in the fashion of the day, but with finger waves to soften the look. Aunty K would

hardly recognize me from the shy, awkward, Russian girl she first knew. A new era demanded a new look, and I felt sure that she would have been proud of me. Besides which, I had many memories that now needed to be locked away, only to be brought out in my very private moments, in my apartment, my safe haven, and on my own.

The store was busier than ever, wealth had been steadily building up in the country following the end of the war. America, although it never had fighting on its soil, had nonetheless been involved from 1917 until the end. Prior to that, from 1914 onwards, it had maintained a position of neutrality, although supplies had been sent, and many people contributed towards relief efforts. There were very many groups in America that did not agree with getting involved, such as the Irish populations, German and Scandinavian immigrants.

One of the difficulties of involving America in the war had been the suspicion that the motives were purely political, and used to gain advantage for the Republican Party. Even the sinking of the *Lusitania* did not sway opinion. It was not until 1917, with the suspected explosions at the Kingsland factory, and the 'Black Tom' boatyard incident, carried out by German saboteurs on American soil, that public opinion started to change. Money was used for war loans to many countries, especially to England and France, and people were encouraged to buy war bonds. All of which were redeemed after the war.

I knew nothing of this at the time as it was never spoken of in the store, and also I kept quiet about my involvement in anything as it had been on the side of Russia. Besides which, everyone thought I was Swedish.

I did, however, notice that there seemed to be more money around as the store had become busier, especially our jewellery department. The two ladies, Betty and Emily, were selling much more of the expensive jewellery, and upturn was reflected throughout much of the store.

One day, Emily and I had to go to warehousing to restock our shelves and showcases. We never really had much time to talk as we were always so busy, and of different generations. But both ladies were very friendly,

2 2

and, indeed, I had been to Betty's home for Christmas dinner. I mentioned that the department was doing well and wondered what the reason might be. Could it be an improvement in everyone's fortunes now that the war was very much behind us...?

She smiled and said, "That is probably a fair assessment; the years immediately following the war were dreadful." She told me that, during the war years, her husband was off fighting, and she had been enlisted, like many women, in the Army Signal Corps as a switchboard operator. Some had also worked for the coast guard. Very few actually went to Europe and those who did served as nurses and ambulance drivers. This had taken place in 1917 and 1918. The emancipation of women had not yet happened in all of the states, and would not be, fully, until after the Nineteenth Amendment to the Constitution had been passed.

We chatted as we walked; I think it was the most conversation we had had since I started working with her. I was really interested as I had also been a nurse, but only knew about the war from the Russian prospective, which, of course, I did not mention. I casually asked, "What happened after the war?" She frowned a little, and then said that 1919 had been a very bad year. The Spanish flu had ravaged Europe, and those troops, who had survived everything, were sent home in their thousands. This had resulted in high unemployment, strikes and, ultimately, riots. I was shocked, I knew none of this. "My husband," she said, "took quite some time readjusting to everything when he got home, as did the whole family."

I had never thought of anything like that, cocooned in my small world where finding my parents had been my only goal. I looked at her, and she looked very upset, so I apologised, and said, "So sorry, I am just interested in the history of my new home." Fortunately, she considered me too young to have known anything of the war.

By the time we got back to the department, laden with boxes of new stock, she was herself again and we exchanged a smile between us, me knowing that it was the end of any such conversations.

Betty was a similar age; I had thought them in their fifties, but realised they must have been younger, and she must have, I supposed, an equally interesting story to tell. However, I decided to leave things be, and not ask any more questions.

My experiences with the Bureau men had made me realise how uncomfortable it was being interrogated, however nicely it was done. Emily and I never spoke of our conversation again, and life in the department went on as before.

One day, Mary came down to our section and, with great excitement, said, "Our dresses are ready, time for a last fitting, then we must make plans for our special night out!"

Chapter Six

Feeling Homesick

The night of the big outing was nearing and we girls had taken home our carefully chosen dresses. These had taken most of our salaries but we had all decided that it was worth the cost as we had all been, for various reasons, feeling down.

I had not really told anyone as to my reasons, but had invented a plausible story. I was very good at this subterfuge, but it was a part of me that I didn't like very much. Fact and fiction were becoming blurred. I needed to speak with my parents.

My father's department was at present recruiting new students, including women, and had a telephone that I knew would be answered by my mother in her capacity as secretary. Firstly, though I would have to get through the main exchange, I assumed the role of a would-be student looking to fulfil a research post.

As expected, my mother answered and I made it clear that there was nothing wrong and asked if I could arrange an 'interview'. We had developed a new name for just such an eventuality. I was to be Anna Gustafson for this purpose.

We arranged a meeting for a week hence, following our big night out. I was to be shown around the faculty and interviewed in the professor's rooms. I would have to be very careful not to be followed. How I hated all of this, but it lifted my spirits to know I would be seeing them. Every time there was a knock on any of the doors in the apartment block, I would become very nervous, expecting it to be the men from the BOI, but, as yet, that had not occurred.

Our big outing had finally come around, and we had decided to go to the Roseland Ballroom, then on to the late-night Cinderella Club. Time at the store seemed to go very slowly. It was the end of the summer, and many of the wealthy families had been away to their holiday homes in the Hamptons, up the coast in New England. Our next busy time would be Thanksgiving.

Three days before our outing, there was a knock on the apartment door. I had not been home long from my shift at the store. My heart sank. There stood the smiling young man. "Miss Neilsson," he said in an official, yet not unfriendly, voice, "please come with me." Outside, the same car was waiting but, apart from the driver, there was no one else in it.

I was shaken and, during the journey, I asked what was the problem. I told myself, silently, not to talk too much as, being nervous, I might say something I shouldn't. He, in turn, said nothing, but stared intently at the road ahead. We stopped at the same large building and alighted. Again, it was a hive of activity, even though it was the early evening. I was taken to an office and met again with the sinister little man.

He asked me how and why I had come to America, and again I gave him the same answers. He seemed more interested in Hannah this time, so I told him how she and I had worked together in Gothenburg, and how when I said I was emigrating, it transpired she also had similar plans. Because of that, we had decided to book a cabin together, sharing the cost. I told him of our time on the ship, about the storm and the eventual docking at New York. All of which he knew, because I believed he was also on the ship.

In New York, we had decided to go our separate ways, she to her relatives in Chicago and me to make a new life in the city. I said that I felt it was right to make my own way, and not just become part of someone else's family. This decision had been made virtually after docking.

"That explains at least one thing," he said. "The address you gave on landing, and why you are not there."

"As I told you previously," I said, "I wanted it to be a new country and a new life. Hannah understood that, and I thanked her for her offer. I saw her off at Grand Central Station that first day and have not seen her since, but I did occasionally write to her via a post office box."

"Yes," he said, "we know."

My nerves had calmed, as what I was telling him was the truth. Aunty K had always said that whatever was being talked about had to have a basis in truth; lies were difficult to maintain and you could be easily caught out. On other matters, it was better to be vague rather than invent scenarios. She was so wise, so I felt confident in what I was telling him.

"Can I ask what this is about? I may be able to help further."

"No," he said. "At present this will do. We just needed to reconcile your papers with the reality of your present situation. You may go," he said abruptly, and again the young man took me down to the car pool.

"What is going on?" I asked. "This is scaring and upsetting me!" He smiled his knowing smile, but said nothing. Obviously I would learn nothing from him.

Back in my apartment, my nerves got the better of me and I sobbed uncontrollably. *Oh, Aunty K, I really need you now.* Later, when I was calm again, I thought it odd that the first person I needed was Aunty K and not my mother. I made a cup of hot chocolate but no food, as my appetite had fled.

My night was not as restless as I had thought, and I arrived at my workstation quite refreshed. Our gang met up for lunch break and, of course, the talk was all about our night out. How lucky they were that this was the only thing they had to worry about. Mary looked at me a few times, and being the most intuitive of everyone, took me to one side and asked what was wrong. "Oh, I am fine," I said, "just a case of homesickness. It has been two years since I saw Aunty K and Carl Gustav and I miss them. It will pass, I am happy with my life here, and do not regret the decision to come here."

She smiled and said, very earnestly, that if I ever needed to discuss anything, she would happily listen, and also be very discreet. Of that, I had no doubt. I thanked her and said brightly that there was nothing of great importance worrying me. This, of course, was not true, so I used all of my acting skills to make it appear so. She seemed happy with my answer, our lunch break ended and we all went back to our respective departments.

I was glad when the day was over and I could retreat to my little apartment. I needed to get myself into a better frame of mind for the outing. Like all of the others, I had been really looking forward to it, and I didn't want any BOI people spoiling it for me. Things in my life would take their course and perhaps this was fate intervening, although why and for whose sake, I just wasn't sure any more.

I wrote Aunty K a very carefully worded letter, as I was now sure that my mail was being scrutinised, and posted it on the way to the store the next day.

Chapter Seven

Our Night Out

The night out had been filling my thoughts for several weeks but, to redress the balance, it wasn't the only time we all went out. We still went occasionally to the tea rooms after the boys had played their tennis matches. We also went to the newly built stadium at the lumberyard site in the Bronx, the home of the New York Yankees baseball team. The two boys had managed to secure tickets for all of us to watch the first home game, in 1923, when the New York Yankees played the Boston Red Sox. It was so exciting, especially when their most famous player, 'Babe' Ruth, hit a home run straight into the right field stands. I had decided at that moment that I really liked baseball and followed the team avidly from then on, whether it be at the stadium, on the radio, or just listening in on the chatter amongst the male customers at the store.

Later, in this year of 1924, the store was to hold the Thanksgiving Parade, and we employees would be dressing up, and there would be floats and bands. New York was certainly very exciting, with many things going on. But first there was our special night out, much needed to lift all of our spirits.

It had been decided that we would go to see the Fletcher Henderson Band playing at the Roseland Ballroom on 51st street and Broadway. It was a place we knew as we had been to see the 'new year ball drop' there, joining in with the countdown to the new year. Always a time of great reflection and excitement, wondering what the next year would bring.

Later we would move on to the Cinderella Club on 48th street and Broadway, number 1600, to see Bix Biederbeck and the Wolverines. September 12th was to be their debut. We had debated whether to go and see Duke Ellington at the Hollywood Club, but decided that perhaps it was a little too sophisticated for us young ones. Bix was young, new and we were all very excited to see him. William and Alice would come to pick me up, Robert, Mary and Lizzie would meet us at the ballroom.

We girls had booked time off from work to be able to get ready in a leisurely manner. I enjoyed being home on a Friday, not that it happened very often. The early part of my day was spent tidying my rooms, and generally making sure my clothes, bag and dancing shoes were ready. Each time I looked at my dress, I got a little shiver of excitement.

The radio played softly in the background. George Gershwin had recently written a new composition called 'Rhapsody in Blue', which was getting a lot of airplay. I liked what I heard. This decade, the 1920s, was so, so, different to the previous one. No wonder people wanted to just have a good time, not knowing when or if the world would turn ugly again.

At the corner of my block was a hairdresser, where I had booked to have my hair finger-waved, to complete my flapper look. On returning home, I was much pleased with the outcome. I could not believe that the image staring back at me from the mirror was the same young girl from the lakeside in Siberia. I looked so grown up, but knew I was still the same inside.

I didn't eat very much – far too excited – and tried to rest a little, but then it was time to get ready. Fresh and clean, I carefully applied what little make-up I had, put on my underwear and stockings before finally putting on my beautiful dress. It looked lovely and I was so pleased with my choice. The colour and the style suited me well. It was worth every cent of the cost. I felt sure that the other girls would be feeling the same, as we had all spent some time making our choices.

I collected my bag and my wrap and went down to the street to await the arrival of William and Alice, who duly arrived, looking equally smart and beautiful in their new clothes. The taxi started off and we all exchanged compliments. We arrived at the ballroom just as Robert, Mary and Lizzie arrived, looking equally resplendent.

There was a photographer in the foyer, so we six posed to have a group photograph done. We would get the prints later from his small shop off Broadway.

Everyone had made such an effort; it was wonderful. We could hardly recognize ourselves. We were ushered into the dimly lit ballroom and taken to our table. The music was already in full flow and there were many dancers on the floor. We had paid for the 'buffet and dance experience' and our table was in a good position for the food, to see the band, and access to the dance floor.

The ballroom was large with silvery-looking pillars around the outer areas, each with lights attached to the tops. I was fascinated. The whole atmosphere was amazing and I felt drunk with the excitement of it all, even though I hadn't had any alcohol. I still felt quite intoxicated with the whole experience. In fact, alcohol, or the lack of it, was a problem as we were in the times of Prohibition and the 18th Amendment. However, as with all things, there were ways and means around things. I'm sure the boys had whisky in their hip flasks, bought from their local pharmacies who could still supply it 'for medicinal purposes'. I didn't ask the girls, but I was happy with the selection of 'soft' drinks on offer.

We ate some food, we danced – shockingly showing our knees as our dresses rode up in the more vigorous numbers. The band was very good, we girls all chose a band member to pretend to flirt with, except for Mary who was deeply in love with Robert. We asked William if anyone had caught his eye but he just smiled, leaving us all to guess. Everyone looked so elegant, the men in their tuxedos and the women in the fashions of the day. I must say that I felt very special, and that we girls from Macy's outshone everyone else. I thought so anyway.

Lizzie and Alice, being younger, were the attention of many admiring glances, dancing as they did with gay abandonment. Even though I was near to their ages on paper, I was, in reality, three years older, although that was still a secret. William asked me to dance, and we enjoyed a few numbers around the floor. We were still friends even though our previous closeness was gone. He took me back to the table, and went off as he saw some friends from the tennis club. I was surprised to feel a tap on my shoulder, and a voice I didn't recognize, asking for the next dance. I turned slowly, and there was the young BOI man, resplendent in his tuxedo. I suddenly felt very shy, but said yes, as a refusal would have been very rude.

As we walked on to the dancefloor, the music changed to a much slower tempo. He gathered me into his arms and we danced, awkwardly at first, but then relaxing into the music. After a couple of dances, he escorted me back to my table, smiled his enigmatic smile and walked away. I was bemused. Mary and Robert were back at the table and naturally wanted to know who it was. I was able to answer honestly that I didn't know, perhaps a customer from the store. Fortunately, they asked no further questions, and I had no desire to tell them about my encounters with the Bureau of Investigation. I was very surprised to see him there, especially with the prohibition laws in force. I told myself that perhaps he was on duty, carrying out an assignment in the ballroom, and it just so happened that I was there too. Many speakeasy establishments had sprung up around the city, each breaking the law in some way or other.

As we were getting ready to leave, to move on to the other club, Robert said he had some news for us.

Chapter Eight

Cinderella Ballroom

We were all intrigued, and promptly sat down again at the table. Robert smiled, took Mary's hand and, in his soft voice, tenderly asked her to marry him.

She blushed furiously – we could tell even in the dim, smoky atmosphere. We all held our breath. He opened up a small box wherein nestled the most stunning engagement ring. With tears running down her beautiful face, Mary whispered, "Yes." The moment hung in the air, then, like a bubble, burst into shouts of joy and congratulations, disturbing the occupants of the other tables, who clapped their approval.

The ring, with its perfect diamond in a flower shaped setting, glistened on Mary's finger, but by far the greatest glow was from Mary herself. She truly shone. The ring so epitomised her, with her gentle, loving, intuitive nature and we were all so happy for them both. Some champagne was conjured up – we didn't ask how – and we sat drinking illegal alcohol in the dimly lit ballroom, celebrating this most happy of moments. We loved them both and had thought for some time that they were the most perfect of couples. A special occasion on a most special night.

Now it really was time to move on to the Cinderella Club – very apt, we thought, as our prince and princess had just openly declared their love.

Robert had been able to get tickets to this venue, knowing many people as he did. The new talent, Bix Biederbecke and his band would be making their debut. It was a strange experience going to any club as they could be the subject of raids at any time – unless the local police turned a blind eye. In my naivety, I knew nothing of this, or, rather, did not want to know. I just wanted to enjoy myself. My goodness, what a night this was turning out to be.

We walked down Broadway until we came to number 1600. The night air was still warm even though it was September and there were many late-night revellers out on the streets. I loved people-watching and looked enviously at the many couples walking hand in hand. I felt quite jealous, even though I was happy for them in their happiness. It made me think of Hans, and in a very strange way of the BOI man. I didn't know what to make of my confused feelings towards him.

I pushed all such thoughts aside and joined in the laughter and talk on the way to the other club. Of course, the main topic of conversation was the proposal. We wanted to know when Robert had planned all of this. No wonder we were encouraged to go all-out, to make a very special occasion even more special. Mary said very little, just smiled her brilliant smile.

We reached the club, showed our entrance tickets, and were taken inside. There was a stage set up at one end of the room and a scattering of tables surrounding the dancing area. Again, it was very smoky and dimly lit, but very atmospheric. The place quickly filled up and we settled into our seats just as the show began.

The Wolverines were a seven-piece band, who had formed a few years earlier in the Midwest. All college boys. They had been slowly making their way north, and this night was to be their first in New York City, where they were to have a residency for a few weeks. We had heard some of their records, so we were very much looking forward to seeing them play live. Bix Biederbecke was their cornet player and he couldn't have been more than 21 years old.

When they started to play, it was magical; you couldn't keep your feet still. I didn't want to dance, just wanted to sit back and watch them, and let the music flow over me.

They played some tunes we had heard, like 'Fidgety Feet', 'Copenhagen' and 'Riverboat Shuffle', all of which had been recorded earlier in the year. They also played 'Big Boy', a new one, yet to be recorded, and then finished as they always did with their signature tune' 'Wolverine Blues', from which they had taken their name.

It was wonderful. The music reverberated all around the ballroom, and the solos by Bix, with all of his improvisations, were amazing. I had never heard anything quite like it; no wonder they were so popular. We were all very impressed. I just kept thinking, *what a night. What a perfect night.* The engagement, our time at the Roseland Ballroom, and now this to finish it all off. None of us wanted it to end.

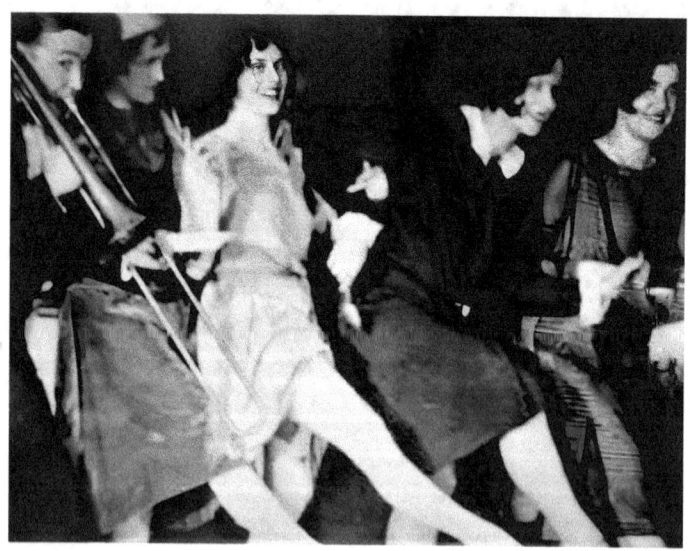

But end it had to, I don't even remember how I got home, but here I was back in my little apartment. I'm sure the others had as much trouble sleeping as I did. I was much too excited for sleep.

However, I must have slept, for the morning came, and the spell was broken. Back to reality, and time to get ready for work.

Chapter Nine

Visit to Cambridge

I had arranged to meet up with my parents under the subterfuge of being a student applying for a research position.

Our special night had taken place and I had had the most amazing time. Now it was back to secrets and paranoia. I got myself ready and set off to work. Once at the store, I went to the staff room and then to my department. I had requested a half day off, so had anyone followed me, I was where I was supposed to be. I did my best to make all seem normal, chatting to my two co-workers and the customers.

The store had become very busy again, and buyers were out in force. It would soon be Thanksgiving, and then Christmas. Betty asked me if I had any plans for the afternoon, but I told her I just needed the rest and would probably go to Central Park for a walk.

She nodded. I liked her, she treated me more like a daughter than a colleague, and I hated not telling her the truth. Emily smiled at me and carried on with her work. At lunchtime, I went down to the basement and left via the warehouse door, stopping at the Hershey's chocolate store on the way. I wasn't aware of anyone following me so, carefully, and in a circuitous route, I made my way to Grand Central Station. I arrived and, within minutes, had bought my train ticket and was settled into my seat.

I had done this trip a number of times and knew the route well. Once at Boston, I changed on to the Cambridge train. My appointment was for 3pm. I arrived in good time. It had to look as if it was for a genuine interview. My appearance had changed greatly from my last visit, as had my English; I even spoke with a faint American accent.

I reported to the desk at the front of the building; fortunately there was a new receptionist who did not know me. I stated my name and whom I had come to see. My mother came for me, and even she hardly recognized the modern young woman before her. She smiled and said in her most business-like manner, "follow me please."

Once away from the reception area, she told me she was happy to see me and that she wasn't really sure, at first, that it was really me. We both laughed, and I started to tell her about our amazing night out. However, before very long we came to father's department, and I was ushered into his office.

Away from all the prying eyes, he hugged me and said he couldn't believe how grown up I looked, and how much I had changed in the months since he had seen me last. I smiled; I was actually 25 years old now, although

I looked younger and could get away with being the 22 that my papers claimed me to be. I gave them my present of Hershey's chocolates.

They were intrigued as to the purpose of the visit, and all the subterfuge. I started to tell them. I told them about the letters from Aunty K and Carl Gustav, and about the visits to the BOI building, and the sinister little man. I told them how worried I was, and about all of the questions they had asked. On talking about it, I realised that he had not asked me about my parents, but had confined the questions to my paperwork, and about Hannah.

My new papers were due to a mistake, I explained, on Carl Gustav's behalf, because he believed me to be younger than I was. My earlier papers had been lost due to the travelling between various countries and the war.

My mother looked alarmed, but father just carried on looking at me and asking various questions. Reluctantly, I told him of the encounter in the Roseland Ballroom with the young Bureau man, and how I wasn't sure if the whole thing had been set up to survey the ballroom for breaches of the prohibition laws, or if I was the subject of interest. Father just nodded but said nothing, so I went on.

Mostly I told him about the sinister little man and how I thought I had first seen him on the ship from Sweden, although, at that point, he was unaware of my Swedish identity. Neither parent said very much and I began to feel very uncomfortable. I didn't think I had done anything wrong, but still I had the awful feeling of letting my parents down. I was so desperate to find them that I didn't think of what the ramifications might be if I did. They had made themselves a new life in America after escaping from Russia, and now it seemed as if I had brought trouble to their settled home.

My father told me not to worry as they had dealt with far worse during their lives and, as there hadn't actually been any mention of them yet, we would have to meet that if, and when, it happened. As of yet, no link had been made between these people and Anna Nielsson of New York City.

I took my leave of them, promising to get in touch straight away if anything changed. On the train home I thought very much about the situation. I loved my parents dearly, but still could not feel a great connection with them. This saddened me, as it had been my goal to find them since I was a young child. Of everyone, I missed Aunty K the most, and even New York, with all of its attractions, could not fill that hole. I began to think about going back to Sweden.

The train jolted and brought me back to the present. Alighting at Grand Central, I changed onto the regional line for the last few stops home. I got off one stop early and, as it was still light, walked home. I was relieved to see that no one was waiting for me, or at least no one I knew. I hurried into my little haven. I had an unsettled night, with many thoughts going through my head.

Chapter Ten

Thanksgiving Parade

I always felt unsettled after a visit to Cambridge and this time the feeling was more acute. Each night I waited for a knock on the door, but the men from the BOI had not appeared thus far.

Mary came into the department and asked me to join her for lunch. I thought it was to tell me about her forthcoming marriage, but it was about me. She was worried and felt that something was deeply wrong. She said that the others had noticed too.

I used the 'homesickness' ploy, and in this case, it was true. I had really felt a strong urge to return to Sweden – my adoptive home – and maybe even to Russia. I missed the countryside, the lakeside, the clear air, more than I had thought possible. Even though I had been in New York four years, the longing for home had become stronger each year.

I asked Mary about their plans for the wedding as she and Robert had decided on a short engagement. They were a well-suited couple. Robert was from one of the older established New York families and was working at the store to gain experience in retail before he took over his father's business. None of us had known this of course; to us he was just Robert from the sportswear department. We knew he had influential friends, but thought no more of that. Mary, too, was from a family steeped in history; her female relatives had all been members of the suffragette movement prior to 1919 when the Women's Bill of Rights had passed into law. Everyone had their secrets and I found it fascinating learning about everyone even after this long time. What were William, Lizzie and Alice hiding I wondered.

Mary and Robert wanted our little gang to be an integral part of their ceremony as bridesmaids, and William as Robert's best man as he had no brothers to ask. Mary, of course, also had her sisters as her bridesmaids. The wedding was to be in the spring, in April of 1925. I was so happy for her, and a little envious. I put on my best act, assured her all was well with me, and enthusiastically joined in her plans.

After she had gone, in the quiet moments, I started to think more seriously about my life, and where it was going. I thought I caught a glimpse of the young BOI man and my heart sank. Surely there could be no more questions. I looked again, but there was no one there. Was I being too paranoid? Another customer took my attention and I snapped back into professional mode.

The evenings were drawing in, and the store was getting ready for the Thanksgiving rush. Also, it would be time for the big parade, the first one ever held through Manhattan, and all employees had been given roles either on or beside the floats. I was to ride on the one depicting 'the old woman who lived in a shoe'.

One October evening I arrived home to find a letter from Aunty K. I was always excited to get news from where I now considered to be my home – Sweden. It was a long letter so, after my meal, and comfortable in my nightwear, I settled down to read it. The letter was full of news about Carl Gustav and his work, and about her work with the horses. There was a brief mention of other family members, but nothing specific. I had told her that I thought my mail was being read, so we used our special code. Towards the end of the letter, there was mention of Hans. In a previous letter Aunty K had said he was trying to get to Sweden, then on to America. However, there was a problem with this; as he was of German descent, getting papers was very difficult. So, after quite some time, he had given up.

I was disappointed but worse was still in store for me; he had met a young lady in Suvecea, and married her. I sat and stared at the page and read it over and over, my tears dropping onto the paper, smudging the ink. Of course, why wouldn't he marry, it had been four years, with very little communication from me, and then only via Aunty K. How would he have known how I felt about him? He could be forgiven for assuming that my new life was everything I wanted.

I was very upset and with no one to talk to about it, I cried myself to sleep. *Oh, Aunty K, I miss you so much, and now I really do feel alone, and want to come home.* But what about my parents? We had formed some sort of bond, but were still not that close. All of my life it had been my goal to find them, but now that I had, it was not as I had imagined, and the BOI business had not helped. I just didn't know what they wanted from me and, at present, I had absolutely no more to give.

I went to work the next day and gave the acting performance of my life – worthy, I think, of an award or a part in a Broadway play. Our gang all met up in the lunch break to discuss our roles in the Thanksgiving Parade, and I was very glad that I was to sit on one of the floats. Our exuberant pair, Alice and Lizzie, were to be fairy-like creatures dancing alongside the floats. William was to walk at the front dressed as a sword-wielding knight, and Robert and Mary were both on another of the floats.

The rest of October and early November passed by peacefully and I began to relax again into my life. All thoughts of leaving would be set aside, at least until after Mary's wedding. The run-up to the Thanksgiving celebrations was very busy, both in the store and in the preparations for the big parade, this being the first year it was to be held. Even though it was Thanksgiving, it was to be called Macy's Christmas Parade, as it was designed to entice people into the store for their Christmas preparations.

The floats were to have a nursery rhyme theme, depicting Mother Goose, Little Miss Muffet, the Old Woman who lived in a Shoe and Little Red Riding Hood, and, of course, astride the main one was

Tom Turkey. I was to be one of the children who lived in the shoe, and Mary and Robert were on the Red Riding Hood float. All of the floats were to be accompanied by dancers in various colourful costumes, and real animals such as bears, elephants, camels and monkeys, supplied by the Central Park Zoo. What a spectacle it would be, and a spectacle it was indeed.

On the day, thousands of people lined the route from the start at 145th Street and Convent Avenue, all the way down to Herald Square and to the store on 34th and Broadway. There were also four marching bands interspersed throughout the parade, the lively music making everyone want to dance. Many of the female employees were dressed as nursery rhyme figures and danced their way along the route with great energy and exuberance – none more so than Alice and Lizzie. The men were dressed as clowns, cowboys or knights. A police escort led the parade from the start, and at the rear was the final float carrying Santa Claus, or Kris Kringle, sitting on a reindeer-driven sleigh atop a mountain of what looked like ice.

At the end of the parade, the Santa figure was crowned 'King of the Kiddies', and he ascended to a golden throne above the entrance of the store from whence he surveyed the crowd. There was a trumpet signal and curtains were pulled back to unveil the window displaying 'the fair frolics of wonder town', with animations by puppeteer, Tony Sarg.

The whole thing was amazing and from that day onwards, people streamed into the store in their

hundreds to do their Christmas shopping. It was deemed such a success that it was decided that the parade would be held every year. It was certainly enough to make anyone forget their woes.

Part Two
Secrets from the Past

Chapter Eleven

Visitors

The nights drew in and the store was decked out in its colourful, shiny decorations, setting the mood for the Christmas festivities. Again, Betty asked me to spend time with her family, and I gratefully accepted.

Presents were exchanged, and a lovely time was had by us all. I joined the gang for the New Year's celebration in Times Square, then we settled in to see what 1925 would bring for us.

For me, several things happened in the early January weeks. Firstly, there was the big blizzard on January 2nd. So much snow fell – the papers said about 27 inches – unprecedented by any standards. Work crews were out all hours to keep the city running. I was unfazed; having spent my youth in Siberia, I was more used to such things.

When life was more back to normal, the BOI called me into their offices again. The young man and the driver came for me. On our way down to street level, I boldly asked him his name and said that I had enjoyed the dance at the Roseland Ballroom. He nodded and smiled, and said his name was Michael. As we had reached the car, I just smiled back.

This time the questions were more specific; they asked me if I had any relatives in New York, to which I replied, "No." As far as I was concerned, Boston was not New York; it was in an entirely different state. My relatives were, as I had previously told them, in Sweden. This line of questioning worried me as it was the first time it had taken that direction. There was the usual nodding of heads, then I was told I could go home. I was taken to the car where Michael was waiting with the driver. He smiled, and we set off. The driver was a different person to the usual one and paid no heed to me. He was, I think, unaware that Michael and I had met before. The journey was in silence but, as it was late, Michael said he would see me to my apartment door. Once there, he said he had also enjoyed the dance, and hoped to repeat it at some other time.

The following day, I received a letter from Aunty K with news that she and Uncle Carl were coming to America. An amazing surprise, but it was not just to see me – for Uncle Carl it would be in a working capacity and he would be travelling to Colorado. However, Aunty K would be staying in New York for a few weeks. I was intrigued, but my overriding emotion was one of pure joy. I had missed her so much, and to see her again so soon made me very happy.

The work that Uncle Carl was involved in was to look at plans – a viability study – for the building of a type of hydroelectric facility somewhere in Colorado. This was, of course, his area of expertise as he and his family had been instrumental in the building of the hydroelectric dam complex, near his hometown in Sweden. Apparently, he, and other European experts, had been invited to America to take part in the feasibility studies. A board of engineers had been commissioned to review all proposals for the new structure. An idea apparently first mooted in 1922. It was all a bit technical for me, but the part about Aunty K being in New York was just wonderful.

I immediately started making plans in my mind as to how I could accommodate her in my little apartment, where I could take her, who I could introduce her to, including a very carefully planned visit to Boston. She already knew about the BOI men, but she was now a Swedish citizen, so there shouldn't be any trouble with her papers.

They would be coming in early February. I couldn't wait to tell my friends and also to see if I could get some time away from work so as to spend time with her. I was to be allowed the odd day here and there, which was good; Aunty K was very self-sufficient and could, I was certain, find things to occupy her. New York had many attractions as I had found to my delight, so I had no worries about her being entertained whilst I was at work.

I told my friends about the visit and they shared in my excitement and joy. Mary said that it was just the tonic that I needed and asked if they would still be in America in April, when the wedding was due. Sadly, I doubted it, but it was nice to know that they were invited. Betty and Emily were happy for me too and even some of the regular customers noticed a lightness in my step. I was so happy, and I told anyone who asked about the visit. The weeks of January passed so slowly. I hoped that the BOI people would be in touch so that I could tell them of the visit before they told me, knowing that they intercepted my mail.

True to form, Michael appeared one evening and escorted me to the building. Again, I was asked if I had any relatives in America, to which my answer had always been no. However, this time, I told them an aunt and uncle were coming from Sweden the following month. My uncle would be working on a government contract for several weeks, and my aunt would be staying with me.

My intention was, I said, to show her around the various attractions of New York. I think they realised how excited I was, after four years of not seeing them.

Even the little man seemed satisfied and they sent me home. It was an exercise, I'm sure, to see if my information was the same as what they already knew.

I thought February would never come but, at last, it did come, and I made ready to meet the ship. By coincidence, it was the SS *Drottningholm*, the one that I had arrived on. However, it had since been reengined, her superstructure enlarged and completely refurbished. She would also be arriving at Pier 97. I arrived early, so excited. They, of course, would be travelling first class, so all of their paperwork would have been checked before landing so hopefully my wait would not be too long.

Finally, I saw them coming down the gangway. What must they have thought when this short-haired, modern-looking miss launched herself at them? My appearance had much changed over the time, keeping up with the fashion of the day, so it took a few seconds for them to realise that it was me. I was almost hysterical with delight. I had thought that they would stay with me, but they had decided to stay in a hotel.

On reflection, that was a much more sensible idea; my apartment was much too small for three of us, and even though I liked its location in Lower East Village, off Orchard and Rivington, it was a very poor area and very noisy. However, I loved it. Aunty K would stay with me once Carl had gone.

I went with them to the hotel – called The Astor, a large and imposing building – and into the reception area. My word, what a place; it took my breath away. I had never been inside any of the really big hotels. Being wealthy certainly had its perks.

After they had been shown their suite, and their luggage installed, they decided to have a look around, with me in tow. What a place; there were public rooms, a palm garden on the lower level, several themed ballrooms, various restaurants with exotic-sounding menus, and on the top of the building was the most amazing roof garden with an observatory and bandstand, hosting the Fred Rich Orchestra. I had never seen anything like it; no wonder they wanted to stay here.

They were very wealthy people; a fact that I had forgotten because to me they were just Aunty K and Uncle Carl.

Chapter Twelve

A Surprise Encounter

The first few days had been spent looking around the city and Uncle Carl catching up with people who he knew through engineering circles. He had not been introduced to my father, even though he knew of him. As yet, no connection had been made; that would come later. He would be coming back so there would be time for savouring the delights of New York before he and Aunty K returned to Sweden.

Once he had gone to Colorado, Aunty K moved in with me and she and I settled back into our easy way of being together; it was almost as if there had been no intervening years. I had work, but I had taken her to various places so that she could fill her day until my work was done. She would often come to meet me and we would walk down Broadway to my apartment.

She especially loved Central Park, with its walkways, the lake and the zoo. She would have preferred the animals to be roaming free in their natural habitat, but was pleased to see that they appeared well cared for. On my days off we would wander around the market, reminding us of the ones we had seen on our travels, especially the large Moscow market. She was the only person I could speak to about such things, and I thoroughly enjoyed our reminiscences. We revived a simplified form of Romanian in case there were any eavesdroppers.

I had introduced her to my friends, who all thought her to be Swedish. She enjoyed speaking with Alice who was originally from Sweden. Like everyone else who met her, they were entranced by her. She was drawn to gentle Mary, and listened avidly to her wedding plans, and plans for the future.

Being February, it was still very cold and we would spend time ice-skating. I wished that she could stay forever. I had telephoned my mother and asked if we could meet in Central Park as we had done when I first came to America. I said I had a surprise for her, but we must be very careful and meet as if by accident.

We set a date, and I could hardly keep my excitement in check. It had been many years since the sisters had seen each other. I told Aunty K that we were going to the pavilion in the park for ices. Many children were out with their toboggans as school had finished for the day. Aunty K and I walked slowly through the park, chatting in our easy way; it was so good to have her here.

Up along the pathway I could see a lone figure huddled up on a bench. As we neared, the figure turned and, on seeing me, lifted her hand in a half wave.

Aunty K stopped and looked towards me, but I walked on as if I had seen nothing. After some moments we reached the bench and I stopped and sat down. I had told neither my mother nor Aunty K of this meeting, so it was a complete surprise.

There was a strange silence as the two women stared at each other and, as recognition dawned, there were tears of joy as they hugged each other. It was a very emotional meeting. I left them and went to buy the ices. When I came back, I didn't know what language they were speaking, but it was in the warmest tones. There was so much to catch up on, so we all went to the Grand Central railway station to sit in the warmth. I didn't feel it was safe enough to go to my apartment, besides which, my mother had to get her return train.

They talked quickly, trying to fill in all of the years that had passed, what had happened in their lives, and how it was that we were all now in America. They were like girls again, especially when they spoke of their home back in Russia. They smiled at me occasionally and I was happy to let them reminisce, especially as I knew that Aunty K would tell me later, at home.

There was just not enough time for all to be said so another meeting was arranged, next time in Cambridge, to meet up with my father. I wasn't sure if I would go, having only recently been, and of course still being of interest to the BOI. However, I would be able to give Aunty K detailed travel instructions and she, being a seasoned traveller, would have no difficulty following them.

Mother left and we took the subway home. We spoke little, but once inside the apartment, the excitement burst free. "Aunty K, did I do the right thing?" I asked.

"Oh yes, it was the most wonderful surprise." she said.

"I think you will have to meet up alone next time; I can't take the risk of being followed, especially as I don't really know why," I said. She nodded and gave me her wise, all-knowing look. "You must be so happy to have seen your sister." She smiled her brilliant smile and I felt so happy for her.

It was such a contrast to how I had felt. I wanted to tell her how difficult it had been for me, how I hadn't been able to make a strong bond with my mother, the initial excitement and then a feeling of almost disappointment as I couldn't relate to the two people who were my parents. I wanted to tell her how guilty I felt, particularly as so many other people had been involved in all of the subterfuge, and that it had made my relationships with other people difficult too. However, I said nothing, and just smiled back at her, not wishing to spoil her happiness.

I was eager to know what had happened in the years between, but Aunty K said there hadn't been enough time to discuss very much except their childhood, which I knew about. I would have to be patient until after she had been to Cambridge.

We made our evening meal and afterwards sat drinking hot chocolate, just as we had done outside the caravan, on moonlit nights, with the gentle breathing of Hercules in the background. We were both quiet in our reverie, and many miles away in our thoughts.

The next day a letter arrived from Carl Gustav, telling her a little about his work, and that he would be coming back to New York. She would then be moving back to the Astor Hotel.

Chapter Thirteen

News from Colorado

Aunty K read and reread her letter from Carl, just as I had done with every one that she had sent me. Although addressed to me, we both knew that it was solely for her. It was good to see her so happy. Her life with Stephan was not forgotten, but she was able to have happiness for a second time. I felt a little envious; none of my would-be relationships had worked out, but I was still hopeful. I suppose that Mary's wedding had brought things more to the fore. I told myself to put aside such negative thoughts – Aunty K had taught me better than that – and to look for the positive in everything.

And here she was, in my apartment, her eyes shining with happiness for Carl, for me and for meeting up with her sister after so many years. It was sad that Aunt Aninya had died as that would have made the reunion complete. There were plans in place for the sisters to meet up again, and who knows where things would go from there. So the mood in the apartment was one of great positivity, as it always was with Aunty K.

The letter was full of news which may or may not have been read by the BOI people – who could tell? I wasn't quite sure if that was a legal practice, but then the agency was a law unto itself. Carl, or Uncle Carl to me, had been working hard in his role as an advisor, along with the other engineers, on the feasibility and practicalities of harnessing the waters of the Colorado River, though for what and why, he gave no details. The project was already a couple of years into the general planning stages, but the fine details needed to be worked out. There was much that needed to be taken into consideration – things like location and all of the attendant facilities such as a railway line and accommodation for the workers and their families.

All of this information was just given in outline with little detail as the project was not universally known of and Carl was also aware that the mail may be intercepted and read. He was in a very good position to be of technical help having built a similar complex near his home in Sweden. Various locations had been looked at, and one had been chosen as it fitted more of the criteria. He did not say where. There would have to be many more studies, permissions and money raised before there could be any thought of the work commencing.

Aunty K studied the letter; it was clear that Carl would be away for some time yet. I knew that she liked being with me, but also that she missed Carl very much. Still, it would give us time for the Cambridge visit, which we had to plan most carefully because of the continued BOI interest. I began to wonder if there was more to my parents' flight from Russia than I knew – after all, it had been more than twenty years now. What could be that important?

The weather had improved – still some snow but nothing like the early January weather – so we decided to go ice-skating on one of my days off. There were a few rinks around, mainly built on the lakes. We decided to go to the one in Prospect Park. The street cars were running, their routes being kept clear of the snow. A red ball would be raised on the front of the trams. It was a way of letting people know that the ice was deep enough for skating purposes. The balls had been on view for several days, so we felt it would be safe to go.

The old boathouse at the lake had been converted to a skate house where you could hire skates for 25 cents and also get coffee and snacks. What fun we had. I had recently been with the gang, but for Aunty K it had been a while so she needed some time to steady herself and get a feel for it again. Once out on the ice we let go of all of our worries and joined the other skaters swirling around the rink. It was exhilarating though cold, but that didn't matter; we would have coffee and pastries to warm us when we finished. Aunty K never ceased to amaze me; when she was happy, she shed years and looked young again as she did now, twirling around the ice. I felt that I was the older one with all of the worries on my shoulders.

Later in the skate house, we sat and talked in our old familiar way. I tried not to think of her leaving again when Carl came back to New York.

Once home in my little safe haven, I spoke to her about all of my fears and doubts. I told her how upset I was about Hans, but also happy about his marriage.

Emotions are strange things, pulling us in all directions. I also told her about Michael, the dance and my very confused feelings about him. I told her too that I really had no idea what was going on with my father and mother, and that even though I had tried, I couldn't get close to them. My whole life's purpose seemed irrelevant now and I felt adrift with it all.

She was her usual calming self, her gentle voice washing over me. She could not change the situation about Hans, but from what little information she had, he was happy, and his life was not too damaged by the war.

As for Michael, that I would have to work out for myself. Did I think he was genuine, or was it a way to my father? Did I trust him enough with any of my true information? Very difficult questions, for which I had no answers. Until I knew why my father was of interest, if indeed he was, I would not be able to work things out with Michael. He had paid me some attention but, she said, I must not confuse gratitude for love. As for the business with my parents, perhaps when she had been to Cambridge, things would be clearer. She was so wise and I had missed her so.

Chapter Fourteen

Family Ties

I had decided that I wouldn't go to Cambridge, so armed with specific directions, Aunty K set off for the pre-arranged meeting.

I was at the store and would spend the day fretting, until I was sure that she was home again. I tried hard not to worry – after all, Aunty K was a very organised lady, with an inbuilt wandering spirit. Also, her sense of direction had been honed after many years of travelling with the fair.

The weather had improved now that it was March, the blizzards of January far behind us. The store would soon be showing its spring ranges, and we on the jewellery counter would be busy again with all of the spring and summer weddings. Although I don't think any excuses were needed for the young men to buy gifts for their sweethearts.

Emily had decided to retire in the summer and Betty was encouraging me to apply for the more senior position. I had the experience, I just wasn't sure if I wanted to stay in America that long, not that I told her that. Aunty K was still staying with me, and we had slipped back into our old comfortable way of being together, and I was dreading her going back to Sweden.

It was becoming a very emotional decision when really I needed it to be a more practical one, as I couldn't just live off Aunty K and Uncle Carl for the next years. Also, I was now, in reality, 26 years old and unmarried. My dreams of being with Hans had turned to dust.

I had achieved my goal of finding my parents, but along the way I had lost most other things in my life. I loved living in New York but it never really felt like home. I liked my friends so a great deal of thinking needed to be done before I made any decisions. Also, the troubling thoughts about Michael were not helping the situation.

The early morning journeys to work on the overhead railway were crowded, and I spent the time staring out of the windows. I noticed the water storage tanks perched on the tops of the buildings, standing quietly like rows of soldiers guarding the people of New York. I thought what an amazing idea it was, so simple and providing water for washing, drinking and for use in fires. There must, I supposed, have been some on my building too, I had just taken the water for granted. Funny what you think about when there is time to just stare out of the windows. I felt much calmer once I reached the store.

After my, thankfully, busy day, I wandered home to find the apartment in darkness. I immediately started to worry as I had expected Aunty K to have returned the Russian way of working, he knew that it would be very unlikely that any replacement plans would be much different to the originals, therefore making his much more viable.

Even though he had made his home in America, his heart still belonged to Russia. He also felt that the plans should never be used in reality by any nation. Who could really be trusted? He had, he told Aunty K, continued to work on them but from a purely academic point of view. Aunty K told me that she could understand that, but felt that it was a dangerous thing to do, particularly as relations between America and Russia were not the best.

I wondered if the BOI had some inkling of this, and this was why I was under surveillance. Had they finally made the link? We decided to put all heavy thoughts aside for the evening and find a nice restaurant.

Chapter Fifteen

Wedding Plans

Carl was due back in the next few weeks, and I had already begun to dread Aunty K leaving. She naturally was very excited to be seeing Carl again. She had enjoyed meeting up with her sister but I think that, like with me, too many years had gone by, too many different experiences, to form any close bond. Instead, we filled our minds with the upcoming wedding, she to make the time go quicker until her reunion with Carl, and me – quite the opposite – to try not to think of her going.

I was hoping that, with the wedding being so close, she and Carl would stay for the celebrations. Although I was desperate for her to stay, I knew, of course, her loyalties now lay with him, whom she loved deeply, and it would be his decision as to when they left. I wanted to be angry with him for taking her away, but I couldn't as I too loved him, my dear uncle and protector. He had made it possible for me to be in America and had financed my first months in New York. I owed him much. I wished I could feel as strongly about my parents, whom I loved and respected in an unconditional way, but it was not the depth of feeling that I had for Aunty K and Carl.

The talk in our little gang was all about the wedding. We were all so happy for Robert and Mary. It was to be a much grander affair than I had realised but, of course, Robert was from New York gentry, not that any of us had known, well except perhaps for William as he had always down-played his background. Mary, too, was from a well-established family and worked at the store because she wanted to, indulging in her love of being with people from all stations in life. Funny how it takes things like weddings to show who people really are.

Me, Lizzie and Alice had been asked to be bridesmaids along with three family and school friends, consequently making it into the bigger affair it was becoming, which I suppose came of them being from old New York families.

Our workdays went on as usual, but each break time was abuzz with wedding talk and plans. We had been shown the patterns for the dresses, and it was time to start with the fittings. As yet, Mary's dress was still a secret. I was glad of the distraction as it meant I didn't have to think about Aunty K leaving.

Carl Gustav was still in Colorado, but it now seemed very likely that he and Aunty K would still be in America for the wedding, their paperwork still valid. Robert and Mary immediately invited them to the celebrations. It made me very happy that my friends had taken them into our little gang, at least for the time being. I, of course, said nothing of my parents.

The wedding venue was to be at the Prospect Park boathouse. A place we all knew well as we had spent many happy hours ice-skating on the frozen lake. It was the most beautiful setting, the Beaux-Arts-style building had been adapted for wedding ceremonies, and overlooked the lake and the surrounding woods.

My time with Aunty K was still happy for both of us. She, of course, was looking forward to the return of Carl Gustav, her excitement plain to see. One shadow on the whole occasion was the inevitable visit of the BOI. It had been a while and I had begun to think that they had given up with me.

Aunty K met up with me most evenings and we chatted all the way home. Turning into Orchard Road, she and I could see the black car outside of the apartment block. My first instinct was to turn and walk the other way but, as Aunty K pointed out, they would probably be watching no matter what time we came back. Besides, she had decided it was time she was introduced to them so, with great trepidation, I walked up to the car.

Michael stepped out onto the sidewalk. I spoke and introduced him to Aunty K. Michael looked at us both, smiled his knowing smile, and held the door open. "There is no need for you to come at this point," he said to Aunty K. She hugged me, then said firmly that she would be coming as she was my aunt and only family in New York. She was very protective. The point made, she stepped into the car.

I was secretly pleased but was, as usual, sorry to involve her in my intrigues. We started to converse in Swedish, but Michael beckoned for us to be quiet. The little man was at his customary desk and was surprised to see Aunty K. She boldly introduced herself and asked what was going on. He was taken aback – I had always been so timid during these meetings – and muttered something about national security. She laughed and asked what possible threat I could be to state security. Her English was just good enough to answer his questions and he seemed particularly interested in Uncle Carl and what he was doing in Colorado. This subject, of course, had its own level of secrecy, as the whole project was still in the planning stages. She told him he would have to speak with government officials regarding that matter. He looked shaken, checked her paperwork and told us to go. He said very little to me.

"What was that about?" she asked once we were back in the apartment.

"I really don't know," I said, "each time I have been they have asked about my papers, but have never really explained why. They used the fact that I had given Chicago as my American address, but had stayed in New York. I have explained why on many occasions. I just don't want to be deported."

"Hmm," she said, "strange that they should be taking so much notice of one immigrant."

I had grown tired of the whole experience, except that it gave me the chance to see Michael, with all of the conflicted feelings that it brought up. I decided to be more honest about Michael, and told her more of my attraction to him. Not that I could really explain; it had no logical reason behind it. She said that I must be very cautious in what I said, especially if I became involved with him in any way. She said that she understood my upset about Hans and did not want me to make any rash decisions. The old uncertainty I had felt during our quest to find my parents had come back, and I didn't like it. New York had felt safe, and now I was very unsettled. Over our hot chocolate, we decided to try to forget about it for now and have a family conference once Carl Gustav came back.

Next day at the store I went into actress mode, smiling at the customers, and enthusiastically finalising wedding plans with the girls.

Chapter Sixteen

Telegrams

There was a knock on the door – most unexpected on a Saturday and so early. Aunty K and I were filled with trepidation. Standing in the hallway was a dark figure we could just make out through the small pane of glass in the door. With shaking hands, I opened the door. It was the mailman with a telegram from Uncle Carl. What a relief. What must that man have thought about the look of horror on my face when I opened the door. I thanked him and took the paper back inside the apartment.

Aunty K was in the kitchen and, for a second, I saw fear in her eyes as I handed her the telegram. Mostly this form of communication was used when something was wrong. However, in this case, it was joyful news. Carl Gustav would be coming back in two days' time, and she was to rebook a suite at the Astor where they had stayed on their arrival. I looked at her happy face as my own emotions tumbled about inside my head. This would mean the end of our time together, which I had enjoyed beyond measure. I was both happy and sad; happy for her and sad for me.

His contract had come to an end and he would be back in New York the following Wednesday. He would send details of which train in another telegram. Her eyes shone when she was happy, and she certainly was the most beautiful person I knew. I waited until I was alone before my tears fell. Mary was the only other person who shared some of Aunty K's qualities and at this moment I longed to speak to her. However, this was not possible. Besides which, she had her own joyous occasion in the offing.

I gave myself a good talking to and re-emerged from the bedroom. I went to Aunty K and gave her a really big hug. She told me that when she and Carl had come to America, they had decided to stay for a short while after the contract's end to go sightseeing. Consequently they would be able to stay for the wedding. That, at least, was of some comfort to me.

My workdays passed quickly, the second telegram arrived and the suite was booked. Carl's train was due to arrive early evening, so I was able to go with her to the station. He had said to meet in the booking hall; a place I remembered well from when I arrived with Hannah, full of excitement about our new lives in America. I was still as impressed with the building as I had been then, as was Aunty K. There was so much activity; people everywhere moving like worker ants, rushing to their destinations. We found some seats and waited.

When at last she saw him, her enthusiasm just bubbled over. This was my calm, organised Aunty K in an absolute well of excitement. I longed to feel like that about someone. There were hugs all around, then a trip in a taxicab to the hotel. I waited in the foyer whilst they changed for dinner. They were longer that I expected but, on reflection, that was not surprising. I spent my time watching people come and go. We decided to eat in the hotel. Uncle Carl was clearly tired and did not speak much, so very soon after the meal I was sent home in another taxicab. My little apartment felt very empty, so I consoled myself with a hot chocolate and went to bed.

The arrangement was to meet the following day, after work. The day could not go quickly enough. As the nights were getting lighter, we spent some time seeing the sights of New York. We wandered into Central Park for the last hour of daylight, and sat on a bench overlooking the lake as the sun was going down. I was eager to hear of Uncle Carl's experiences in Colorado.

Mostly, he said, it was a guarded secret, classified, but he could tell us a little information. He had been involved in the search for an ideal location for an engineering project, able to support a large structure and all attendant facilities, but was not allowed to say what, where or when. He and the other guest engineers had been invited to share their knowledge and expertise. His work in Sweden had qualified him in international circles. When he spoke of his work, his enthusiasm was evident, and when he looked over at Aunty K, love and respect flooded from him. He had missed her, and she him.

The conversation turned to the wedding. Yes, they would be honoured to come, and that made me very happy. I would be meeting Mary at the end of the week to finalise arrangements. Something to keep me busy and to put off thinking about their eventual departure.

Carl wanted to know about Aunty K's visit to Cambridge, and expressed a desire to meet with my father. My father had contributed to several journal articles and his name was known in engineering circles. His main area of expertise, since coming to America, had been chemical engineering, but he had a historical interest in mechanical engineering. To me, it was if Carl was talking about a stranger as I had still not made a real connection with either of my parents. It is strange that things that you want most in life do not always turn out to be the best ones. Often, what happens along the way is of much more importance.

Arrangements were put in place for a visit from Aunty K and Uncle Carl. Again, I opted to stay at home, and I had work anyway. The day they went to Cambridge, I met up with Mary and the other girls to talk about dresses and general arrangements. The wedding was to be in four days, so all of us girls needed to know our roles. Alice and Lizzie were so excited as we went for our final fittings. I did my very best to be happy and enthusiastic.

The dresses were in a subtle peach colour, flapper style, made by seamstresses in the area where I lived. There were long gloves and hairbands with small bunches of silk flowers on the sides. Once dressed, I have to admit that we all looked really lovely. The other three bridesmaids – Mary's relatives – were also there, and when we lined up together the effect was stunning. We were all intrigued as to what Mary's dress would be like, but we knew that, without a doubt, she would look absolutely beautiful.

Chapter Seventeen

The Wedding

The day of the wedding dawned and was a clear crisp day, reasonably warm and thankfully dry.

Aunty K and Uncle Carl had booked me a room in their hotel so we could all get ready together. It was so exciting; the only other wedding I had been to was theirs. I woke early and we all went to the dining room for a sumptuous breakfast. There was so much variety, as was befitting such a luxurious hotel. What a life Aunty K and Uncle Carl led; having wealth certainly had it's compensations, and this breakfast was one of them.

I went back to their room to finish getting ready. Mary's sisters were helping her at their family home, so I wouldn't see her until the ceremony. I luxuriated in the big bathtub, then Aunty K helped me get dressed. The dress was as lovely as I remembered. Lastly, Aunty K fixed the headband into my hair. Although big hats were the tradition for bridesmaids, we had all opted for the simpler headbands. She stood back with glistening eyes and told me how beautiful I looked. I felt wonderful. Now was her turn to get ready; she had bought a beautiful dress from Macy's – the very height of fashion – and looked absolutely stunning.

Uncle Carl had gone to my room to get ready and came back to the suite ready to escort, as he said, his two favourite ladies. Looking at them both together, it was very easy to see why they were so suited to each other; the mutual love and respect shone from them. I wished with all my heart I could meet someone and be that happy. There was still time – Aunty K was in her 30s when she met Carl, so I was ever hopeful.

Carl hired a limousine to transport us to the boathouse. We arrived and met up with Alice, Lizzie, and Mary's childhood friend, Cordelia. Mary and her sisters would arrive later. William was there, looking very smart in his suit, and, of course, a very nervous-looking Robert, resplendent in his morning suit. A number of guests, including members of both families, were already there and had taken their places in the beautifully decorated white and cream ballroom, up on the first floor where the ceremony was to take place. Mary and Robert had opted for a modern civil ceremony, later to have a blessing done at her local church.

There was a quartet set up to one side of the room, playing softly in the background, and many tables set up around the room. The seating plan had been very carefully arranged so that, apart from the main family table, there was a random mix to allow people to get to know each other. When my bridesmaid duty was done I would sit with Aunty K and Uncle Carl. Then, once the ceremony was finished, the ballroom had been hired for the rest of the day and evening.

We bridesmaids waited outside for the arrival of Mary and her sisters, Agnes and Sarah. Mary duly arrived and our breath was taken away by the vision we saw before us. Her dress, which had been made by one of New York's best seamstresses, was of a quite simple design, white, two tier, to mid-calf, the under-layer silk, and the top tier made from a light, free-flowing material. A simple, long pearl necklace adorned it. She wore T-strap shoes of a pale peach colour and long gloves to her elbows. Her natural beauty shone forth and a dress with fussy adornments would have detracted from her. To complete her look, she wore a very long veil and Juliet-style cap, affixed to either side of her head with silk flowers which were reflected in her shower bouquet. This consisted of small white orchids, gardenias, lily of the valley, orange blossom and six pastel peach roses, one representing each bridesmaid. I don't think I have ever seen anyone look so beautiful and serene, and sublimely happy.

The music started, we picked up her veil and, with her two sisters leading the way, we walked into the room. There was a collective gasp as the full splendour of her came into sight. Robert could not resist turning around, and the love that cascaded from him was plain to see. William gave him a supportive smile.

We found our places and the ceremony began. As befitting both of them, the ceremony was beautiful, every word. The vows were exchanged and then they were man and wife. In the time between the ceremony and the meal, we all made our way for photographs to be taken; a fairly new innovation favoured by the elite to record important happenings. The double staircase made the perfect backdrop.

Outside, the sun had come out and the white terracotta building, based on the Sansorvino Library in Venice's St Mark's Square, glowed in the sunshine.

More photographs were taken from the ground floor steps out to the patio, and the arcade facing the Lullwater section of the lake, and the Lullwater Bridge. The bronze lamps with their dolphin motifs were not yet lit but, come darkness, they would be shown to their best advantage. It was the tradition for the bride and groom to have pictures taken under the bridge. I don't think I had ever experienced anything so lovely.

Back inside, the rest of the day went by in a whirl. There were people present for the meal, which I couldn't remember but knew that I enjoyed it, speeches from friends and family, and then people wandered about the location, the building and the surrounding woods.

The evening festivities would start soon, when many more friends would be arriving. Also, an eight-piece band would be playing. This would really please the young ones present, especially Alice and Lizzie who just lived for dancing. Aunty K and Uncle Carl enjoyed their day, reliving their own May wedding five years earlier.

Darkness began to fall and the lamps lit up all along the front of the arcade, showcasing just what a beautiful building the boathouse really was. The elegant Tuscan columns the length of the building, and the balcony on the first floor, were utilised by many couples enjoying the views and the reflections on the lake.

There was a buffet laid on for the evening guests. I couldn't eat a thing, still too excited by the day's events. The band was good and reminded me of our nights out and, as was customary, the ushers asked the bridesmaids to dance. The floor remained crowded for the whole evening. I decided to sit down for a rest. Aunty K and Uncle Carl, lost in each other's arms, stayed on the dancefloor.

I looked around the room. There were so many people – some sitting, some dancing – when suddenly a familiar figure caught my eye. No, it couldn't be, but it was. Michael was sitting with a crowd of people at another table. I sank down in my seat, hoping he hadn't seen me. I also hoped that Aunty K, who was on the dancefloor, had not seen him either. Lizzie and Alice came back to the table. Nonchalantly, I asked if anyone knew the young man over yonder. Lizzie giggled. "I do," she said, "he is Michael Gallagher, from my neighbourhood. He is stepping out with that singer, Eliza Worthington. She sings with one of the orchestras." She giggled again, then said, "You had better not have eyes on him, apparently she is a very jealous creature and would not hesitate to cause trouble."

"Oh no," I said, keeping my voice as steady as possible, "he just looked familiar. A customer perhaps, yes that must be it, a customer." Fortunately, Lizzie by this time had looked away, eager to continue dancing with Mary's cousin, the very handsome Xander Berksley, an up and coming businessman at the stock market. Alice wasn't really listening.

Aunty K and Carl arrived back at their seats, so I whispered in her ear about seeing Michael. Though I could not keep the disappointment from my voice, she asked no questions. However, it did answer my question about the Cinderella Club – he must have been on assignment. I managed to avoid Michael for the rest of the evening.

Chapter Eighteen

Trouble in Cambridge

Having never received a telegram before the ones that came from Colorado, now suddenly there was a third one. It was for Carl Gustav to go to Cambridge. What was happening? We had all been so careful, yet this piece of paper did not bode well.

I went to the hotel and delivered the news. Aunty K and Uncle Carl had already started their preparations for their return to Sweden, albeit in a few days. They were both perturbed and intrigued. What could be so urgent as to warrant a telegram? They would go early the next day. Again, I had work, so it was decided I would stay and keep to my normal routine. Whatever the problem in Cambridge, Aunty K and Uncle Carl were in the best position to sort things out.

I was looking forward to meeting up with the girls to relive our wedding experience, and also I had a lot of thinking to do about Michael. I liked him, but had no wish to endanger my parents in any way, and also the revelation regarding his girlfriend had squashed any thoughts of a future with him, on any level. I had never had to deal with fiery, jealous girlfriends, and I certainly didn't want to now.

I had reflected on much since the wedding, which, although being a very joyous occasion, stirred up many feelings within me – homesickness being the major one. But herein lay a problem, homesickness for where? Russia? Some news had filtered through, none of it sounding particularly good, with all the top government men vying for prominent positions. Lenin, we had heard, had died in 1924, and it seemed likely that Josef Stalin was about to emerge as overall leader. I wasn't sure that I wanted to go back to that. Russia wasn't even called Russia any more; it was, since 1922, the Union of Soviet Republics (USSR). My happiest memories had been in Romania with Aunty K, but she now had a new life in Sweden. I felt so unsettled.

Mary and Robert had gone to visit relatives in New England as part of their honeymoon. Back in work, Betty and Emily were eager to know details of the wedding, and I was happy to oblige. Naturally they wanted to know all about Mary's dress, our bridesmaid dresses and the venue. I described everything the best I could, especially the wedding dress, the simplicity and the absolute beauty of it. Mary, although a modern young woman, had an air of timelessness about her. The whole occasion reflected not just her personality, but that of Robert too

The lunch break neared, and two very excited young ladies came to meet me. Lizzie and Alice were still reliving the whole experience and their enthusiasm spilled out across the jewellery counter. Betty and Emily smiled and nodded. The girls' excitement was infectious, and even I was lifted by it.

Later I waited anxiously in my apartment for news from Aunty K and Uncle Carl. There was a knock on the door and I rushed to open it but, to my surprise, it was Michael. I stared at him, unable to say anything. He looked very uncomfortable and just stood in the doorway. Eventually I was able to ask what he wanted. "Can I step in?" he asked. I hesitated, then said yes, although I did leave the door open. "I have come to apologise," he said, "for ignoring you at the wedding." So he had seen me. "I was there with my young lady, Eliza, and she does not like me speaking with other ladies." I had been glad really that he hadn't spoken to me as I did not wish to let the others know how I knew him, so I thanked him and stood awkwardly in my hallway. He smiled and said, "Well, until next time." He turned and was gone. I didn't know what to think – what a very odd encounter. Perhaps it did matter to him what I thought, or perhaps not. The people from the BOI were very adept at hiding their true feelings and motives. Perhaps he was checking up on Aunty K. Whatever the reason, I felt very wary of him.

I decided that a hot chocolate was my best option – always my comfort in times of stress. I still had yet to hear any news from Cambridge. At last, there was a sound on the stairs and it was Carl, asking me to accompany him to the hotel where Aunty K was waiting. It was only 8pm, but it felt like many hours since I had finished my working day. I was consumed with curiosity regarding the visit.

Carl began by saying that the sense of urgency in the telegram had really worried him. Being married to

Aunty K made him part of our family, with all of the intrigues that came with that status. However, only he had gone to Cambridge. My mother had met him from the train and taken him to where they lived at the edge of the campus. Father was in a state of flux, and from the disarray of the house, was in the midst of packing up. Once Carl had been refreshed, my father began.

He had gone to his class as usual when one of the new research students had asked to see him alone. Once classes were finished and the other students had left, they sat down for their talk. At first, said my father, it was all very general, relating to the research topics, but then the questions started to take a different turn. The student started to ask about Russia and what did he think about the regime there. My father had replied that it was of little interest to him, being from Scandinavia. Sweden, in particular, was classed as a neutral country, and also he had been in America since 1902. The student smiled, then mentioned Irkutsk, and said that his father had worked there at the turn of the century.

Alarm bells had begun to ring for the professor. Known here as Frederik Olaf, his real name of Sergei had not been used for decades. He had kept his voice as steady as possible, and feigning interest asked the student about his father and his work. The student apologised and said they had seen a newspaper article regarding some reward ceremony, and his father thought that he had recognised the professor, but clearly he was wrong.

The talk ended and the student left. My father had been very rattled, but hoped it hadn't shown. He had then decided to talk it over with Carl Gustav. Who would benefit from any information that my father may still have?

Carl had persuaded my father to talk to him about the papers that had been kept hidden for so long. The ideas were indeed still relevant; technology hadn't moved on very far, and the content was still current. Carl had been shocked at what he had heard. Obviously some tweaks would need to be applied to make the plans of any practical use, but the theory behind the science was of a sound basis. He could see why both the Americans and the Russians would want ownership of them.

Carl, of course, was not specific in telling Aunty K or me what the plans actually contained. My father would have to make some very hard choices. Should he destroy the documents – putting science back many decades – should he give them to the American scientists, or back to his Russian counterparts? Whatever the outcome, it would need to come with many airtight guarantees.

Carl had said that he didn't envy his choices. To give them to the Americans would mean he would be forever cut off from his homeland, where there was still a small desire to return. But what little news did come through from the USSR was not good, with various leaders vying for position, especially the particularly ruthless Josef Stalin. Thoughts of what the information may be used for in such a regime did not bear thinking about. Carl had reluctantly left, leaving my father with his very hard choices.

Chapter Nineteen

Family Conferences

After talking with Uncle Carl, it was plain that some serious decisions needed to be made. He and Aunty K were due to return to Sweden but had managed to extend their stay in America.

Once back in my little haven, I fretted and worried that my actions may have compromised my parents. Had my quest opened old, buried secrets? I had not really thought about any ongoing consequences to my parents in my desire to find them. At present there was nothing I could do, so taking the sage advice of Aunty K, I went home to carry on my life as normally as I could.

My work was a source of pleasure to me, and so, with my happiest face firmly in place, I presented myself in the department. Emily had now given notice of her intention to leave, and both she and Betty encouraged me to apply for her position. I would have to decide whether I wanted to stay in America; a conversation I had had with myself many times lately. Depending on what decisions my parents made, I could be left in America on my own. Not exactly alone – I had my wonderful friends – but, of course, they could at any time marry. This would all be in the yet unknown future.

The store was busy; it was now May and there had been a spate of spring weddings. Excited brides-to-be, escorted by their young men, choosing the most beautiful jewellery. I couldn't help feeling happy for them, for the promise of what was to come. I was, after all, a romantic at heart.

I noticed a young man standing quietly, looking at the displays. Betty nudged me, so I went over to him. "Can I be of assistance?" I asked softly.

He came out of his reverie and stared at me. I asked again, and was about to walk away when he said, "Oh, yes please." I never liked to push any of the customers; it was counter-productive. They would be much more at ease, and also often spend more, if left unhurried. "I would like to look at the diamond bracelets," he said in a soft but unusual American accent. I brought out a tray for him to look at and as I laid it on the counter, his eyes met mine. They were clear and sparkling bright, of a pale colour which I couldn't ascertain. We smiled at each other. He looked earnestly at each bracelet, then picked one out. A quite simple design, with perfectly cut stones.

"Would you mind trying it on for me?" he asked. I looked across at Betty, but she just nodded so, pushing up my sleeve, he put the beautiful bracelet on me. I had never worn anything like it. It shone, reflecting the store's lights. Each time I moved, rays of rainbow colours bounced from each stone's surface. It was no wonder that these bracelets were so expensive, they must make their recipients feel so loved. I savoured the moment for another second, then he unclasped it. "Yes," he said, "I think that will be perfect." I carefully boxed it up and idly wondered who the lucky girl was who would receive such an amazing gift. The price tag was several months of my salary, which he paid without hesitation.

After he had gone, Betty and I looked at each other and remarked that somewhere there was going to be a very lucky and happy young lady. Emily had been to the stockroom and returned to two smiling faces. None of us had seen the young man in the store before. I suppose he was about my age, or at least the age that the ladies thought I was. We were intrigued; he looked vaguely familiar, yet we couldn't place him. We didn't usually discuss any customers, but that had been such a happy occasion. It had done me good to escape from my current worries, even if it was just for a short time.

Mary had decided to carry on at the store for at least the present. I was glad, I really felt at ease with her, and liked her very much. Lizzie, Alice, Mary and I decided to meet up for lunch. I told them about the sale, but not who the customer was and, apart from Mary, we felt a tinge of envy towards the bracelet's new owner, whoever she was. William arrived and we told him. He tutted at us in mock horror, but joined in the laughter. We all shared in a warm moment, which was what made our little gang so special. We were sorry that Robert hadn't been there. We decided to have another outing, perhaps a picnic in Central Park. I asked if Aunty K and Uncle Carl could come, especially as they would be leaving soon. They were all happy with the suggestion, having met at Mary and Robert's wedding.

Towards the end of our lunch break, Robert appeared. The girls excitedly told him of my encounter and described the young man. "Oh," said Robert, "I think that sounds like the new player the New York Yankees have just taken on, he was in the sportswear department earlier on." He smiled and said, "A rising star from all the stories about him. He has been featured in the *Herald* a few times." We all nodded, no wonder he looked familiar.

We hadn't been to many matches at the stadium for a while, so thought that perhaps it was time to start going again more regularly. The day passed without further incident and a familiar face was waiting for me at the end on my shift. It so reminded me of the times that Aunty K would walk me home at the end of my workday at the shipping office in Brasov, so very long ago. The years dissipated, and I was a teenager again. I felt very nostalgic.

We went to the hotel where Carl was waiting for us, and also the surprise figure of my father. I was shocked to see him in New York. My mother was there too, both of them looking tired and anxious. Since Carl had been to Cambridge, much thinking had been done, culminating in the need for this family conference. I would ordinarily have been excited at this get-together, but the background situation was much too serious, so not exactly a time for celebration.

A meal had been booked in the hotel restaurant to give an air of normality to the proceedings, although I had lost my appetite as I was much too nervous. Who else could be watching, who else could know? Back in the suite, the more serious discussions were to begin.

My mother looked tearful and Aunty K was uncharacteristically quiet. I was bemused, and could not get out of my mind how my parents seemed to have aged in such a short time. The talking, consequently, was left to the men.

Chapter Twenty

Jake

Momentous discussions were being held, and although I was not directly involved, it still affected all of us. My father and mother had arrived from Cambridge and were with Aunty K and Uncle Carl, trying to make the best of a very serious situation. I was going about my normal duties at the store until my input was required.

The store was very busy, and our new spring range of jewellery was out on show. I still thought about the shy young man and the beautiful diamond bracelet, and wondered what had become of both of them. My questions were answered in one respect, as in the following couple of days, the young man reappeared in the store. He again came to the jewellery counter, and this time asked to look at men's watches. He caught my eye, and smiled. "I would like to introduce myself," he said in his soft voice, with just a hint of an accent. However, it was not an accent that I recognized. I had prided myself that I was pretty good at knowing people's backgrounds, but with him I wasn't sure. "My name is Jake Carruthers, just recently moved here," he said, as he looked at all of our name badges.

We smiled and said "Anna, Betty, Emily."

"Happy to meet you all," he said, particularly looking at me. I could feel my face starting to blush under his gaze.

"How can I help you?" I managed to stutter out.

He had come to buy his father a watch. The diamond bracelet had been for his mother. Being straight forward folk, the presents were not to be too ostentatious, hence the simple design of the bracelet. All three of us helped in his choosing and he walked away happy with his purchase and gave a final backward glance to me. The blush on my face and neck deepened to a deeper red. Betty and Emily looked knowingly at each other.

I could not trust in any of my feelings; each man that I thought I could become close to had been involved in circumstances that precluded any such intimacy. I suppose I wanted the uncluttered friendship that I had had with Tomas, my fisherman friend from the shores of Lake Baikal. Of course, we were children then, and adult relationships were so much more complicated.

However, I was intrigued about Jake and the origin of his strange accent. But again, during our lunchbreak meet up, it was Robert who was the possessor of knowledge. "Jake," he said to three very fascinated girls, me, Lizzie and Alice, "was Jacob, who had come to New York from North Carolina, where he had played baseball in the junior leagues. He was a pitcher of some repute."

"But, what of his strange accent?" I asked.

"Oh," he said, "that would be from his background, from when the family emigrated from Scotland."

"Scottish!" That explained it, so we three girls decided right then that we should go to more baseball matches.

Back at the counter, the two older ladies wanted to know if there was any more information on the quiet young man. It was not the store policy to discuss customers, but that did not stop us being curious. We spoke in hushed tones as I told them what I knew.

I didn't speak of this after work time as there was enough intrigue happening, and this seemed very frivolous by comparison. I went to the hotel to see what developments there were. I was met with very sombre faces and from the tone of the conversation, it seemed that I would be getting involved in the proceedings. Father still had not made his decision and, after much soul-searching, had not decided what to do with the blueprints and all of the paperwork. He and Mother would leave to stay with Aunty K and Uncle Carl in Sweden. Frederik, well, Sergei, my father, had decided that there was too much turmoil in Russia to be trusted with such information. However to hand the papers to the Americans would be considered treason. No wonder he looked so stricken and, suddenly, very old. To destroy everything would be a disservice to science. A desperate dilemma.

Once all of the leaving preparations were made, I would also need to make my decision too. I was at a crossroads; I liked my life in New York, my friends and my thoughts of new friendships. I loved Aunty K very much, but she had made a new life for herself with Carl Gustav and my relationship with my parents had stayed much the same as it was at the beginning when I first found them. Finding them had been my life's goal, but now I was content that I had met them and had shared in the adventure with my beloved Aunty K. She had also been able to meet up with her sister after so many years. I had grown up, now making my own decisions, and my decision was that I would stay in America. Sweden was always an option, if I chose it to be.

I had not told anyone of my thoughts yet, but Aunty K, being intuitive as always, knew. She took me to one side and, in her calming voice, assured me whatever I chose would be fine. I was, after all, almost 26 in reality, and old enough to make difficult choices. The one piece of very good advice she gave me was, "Choose for yourself and your life, do not rely on anyone else to fulfil your destiny."

Part Three
Rejoining of the Broken Pieces

Chapter Twenty-one

Parting of the Ways

Life was to carry on as normal, well, as normal as it ever was for my family. Father gave notice to leave to the institute, effective from the following spring.

It was not just the leaving of his post at the university, it was his whole way of life; his home and the few friends that he and Mother had made in Cambridge and Boston. I could not help but feel responsible, but he assured me that they were tired of living a lie, and wanted to live a life where they were not forever looking over their shoulders.

Aunty K and Uncle Carl had left and gone back to their life in Sweden, however it was not the last I would see of them. Carl would be returning the following spring for more discussions in regard to the building of the Colorado project. This would be coupled with any plans set in place for the moving of my parents to Sweden.

How I missed the days when my life was just a series of small adventures, on the road, travelling with Aunty K and Hercules. Of course, I realised that things would never be like that again; they were from a far less complicated but magical time.

My life was very different now. I had had to finally grow up, and I wasn't sure I liked it. It was not at all how I had imagined things, it was still full of many broken parts.

The summer came and Emily retired. I applied for her position and was duly appointed as buyer for the department. It was part of my role to learn about any new trends, attend jewellery conventions and restock our counters with the latest looks as well as continuing the lines beloved of the older customers. It opened up a whole new world for me, and my confidence grew again. I hadn't realised that this was part of Emily's role, and Betty was happy to support me in the post, for which I was grateful. Naturally there was much more responsibility, and a higher salary. This had swayed my decision as to whether to leave or not.

Jake would come into the store on occasions and buy trinkets for some relative or other. He always wanted me to serve him. We had taken on a new member of staff; a young woman of Welsh origin, Vivien Hughes. Her father was a skilled miner and had emigrated with his family to the coal industry in Pennsylvania. When the family had decided to move to Minnesota, she had not wanted to go, and moved to New York instead. She was very personable, and fitted into our section well. She was also a New York Yankees fan, and was very knowledgeable on the subject and would fill us in on all the baseball news. Sadly, the Yankees were having a bad season and had dropped down the rankings, in part due to what the newspapers called 'Babe Ruth's mysterious illness'. We had also been to some of the matches with William, and were sure that the next season would be better.

One day, Jake came in looking more nervous than usual. I thought it must be to do with the team doing badly. If it was, he didn't say. He beckoned me to move over to a corner of the counter and, in hushed tones, asked me if I would walk out with him and take a stroll in Central Park the following Sunday. I was stunned, but heard myself saying, yes. He looked relieved, then said, "Sunday then, 3pm at the main gates."

After he had gone, Betty smiled and said, "I knew he was interested in you."

I blushed, something I had been doing a lot of lately, and said, "I don't understand why, he could have his pick of any of the ladies." Inside I was pleased, although I did wonder why he would choose a shop girl from the city.

When I told the others, they couldn't believe it and I began to think it was all a joke at my expense. Nevertheless, come Sunday, I went off to the park with William and the two girls, Alice and Lizzie, who promised me that if he was really there, they would wander off. He was there and, true to their word, after introductions were made, they walked away. I suddenly felt very shy, but he put me at my ease. He was tall and I felt very protected in his presence. As we walked down to the lake, he asked about me. I still had to be Swedish

Anna, so mostly told him about my time since arriving in America, minus any BOI references. This certainly wasn't the time for the speaking of any secrets.

He told me about playing in the minor leagues, being talent spotted, and brought to New York. This was his second season, although he spent most of the first one on the bench, learning the team's tactics. He was a left-handed pitcher, but he batted with his right. He laughed and said, "It confuses the other players somewhat." I listened to his stories, spoken in the soft, what I now knew to be Scottish accent. He made me laugh and I enjoyed his company. If anyone stared at us during our walk, I didn't notice.

Too soon, we completed our circuit around the park and he put me in a taxicab, with a promise to meet up again. I hoped so, but I was also realistic; he was on the verge of fame and I was just Anna from Macy's. I wondered what he would think or feel, if he really knew the truth about my life. Maybe one day I would tell him.

I arrived home, and was brought down to earth with a bump. Michael was waiting. Now what! I felt vaguely angry with him as I got into the waiting car. As always, he said nothing, just smiled, but, I thought, he did not look as happy as usual. Perhaps he had had words with Eliza Worthington. I always called her by her full name. I suppose, in the beginning, I was jealous of her, but no longer as Jake had begun to fill my thoughts.

In the office, I was questioned about where I had been, and who with, even though I was sure they knew.

They wanted to know how I could possibly know him. I explained about the store and the gifts for his family. They nodded. I was asked if my visitors had left, to which I answered that they had. I had nothing more to tell them, not really knowing what it was they wanted. Strangely, no mention was made of the visitors from Cambridge.

In the car on the way home, Michael asked if that really had been Jake Carruthers. I answered, quite abruptly, "As far as I am aware." In the dark interior of the car, I could not see his expression.

Chapter Twenty-two

Confessions

I didn't really want to speak with Michael; I was annoyed at him and his colleagues for spoiling my lovely day. It wasn't as if they asked anything new, just went over the same ground all of the time. My anger made me bolder. "What is it you want of me, this treatment is upsetting and making me ill."

He was taken aback; I was rarely so forthright but I had had enough of all of the intrigue. He started to say that he could not tell me anything. I cut across his speech and said, "In that case, do not speak to me again." I had reached the end of my patience with the matter. I knew it was really the sinister little man I was angry with, but unfortunately Michael was the only one present onto whom I could vent my frustration. I turned away, and no more was said. Besides, if I was to have any sort of friendship with Jake, I didn't want the BOI involved. The rest of the uncomfortable ride home was in heavy silence. He opened the car door and I went up to my apartment.

Inside, I wept.

The next day, Betty asked me what was wrong as I was unusually quiet and she was worried about me. I decided to be truthful with her – well, to an extent. I told her about the BOI people and how they kept checking my papers, or so they said. This had gone on for a couple of years and it had worn me down. I told her that I didn't really know what they wanted and, on this occasion, the visit had ruined a lovely day out. I told her about the stroll in the park with Jake.

She said nothing at first, then laid her hand on my shoulder and suggested kindly that I go to our rest room as I was visibly upset. Once away from the department, I was able to settle myself again. These were the times that I missed Aunty K the most. Once I had composed myself, I went back to the counter. Betty smiled at me and said quietly, "Don't worry, speak with your friend, Mary, she will know what to do for the best." She was right, of course; Mary was such a calming influence.

The morning passed quietly and the general running of the department took up all of our thoughts. In a strange way it felt liberating to finally tell someone about parts of my life. Betty assured me what had been said would be kept confidential. I was grateful. I sent a message to Mary, asking her to meet me after our shift.

We met up and naturally she was intrigued. We were to walk down Broadway where we would meet up with Robert later. She could see how agitated I was, so we stopped to sit on a bench in Herald Square. I started quietly to tell her about the evening visits to the BOI building, and how it made me feel very nervous. I had come, I said, to America because I felt it would give me a better life. I had not expected an inquisition all of the time. I so wanted to tell her all of the truth, but knew it would put my parents at risk, especially as they were now so near to leaving. I told her what I could, about living in Sweden, then arriving in New York. Again, I was deliberately vague about Romania and Russia. I was uncomfortable about this aspect as I liked Mary and knew she cared about my welfare.

She was quiet for some time, then said, sagely, that she thought things would improve, and that she was sad that I had been dealing with it on my own. She also thought, rightly, that seeing Aunty K and Uncle Carl, and then them leaving, had upset me greatly. She questioned if I really wanted to stay in America, and said that I would need to do some deep and difficult thinking. "Generally," I said, "I am happy here. I like working at the store, I love being with you, my friends, and New York is a fun place to be, with lots to offer." She smiled. "Also, I have met Jake, or rather he met me, and we walked out together on Sunday, and I like him." I said that I didn't suppose it would really go anywhere, but at present, I was enjoying his company. I also told her a little about Michael and that now I felt betrayed by him, although it wasn't actually his fault, it was the job.

She smiled again and asked if I would like her to speak with Robert to see if he could be of any help. I said no, but thanked her. It was enough at the moment just to be able to speak with someone about things. Even with kind, gentle Mary, I was unable to tell her the whole truth. I vowed to myself that if I did ever leave, I would tell her everything.

We walked on, meeting up with Robert. I smiled at him and mustering the little positivity I felt, cheerfully asked him how he was enjoying his new role as supervisor. He was, he said, liking it and it was good experience for him in preparation of taking over his family firm. He and Mary linked arms and I again thought how well they looked together, and how happy. We walked to the nearest subway station then caught the trains back to our respective homes. I felt a little better, but I hoped that I hadn't burdened her with my worries, or put her in any jeopardy in regard to her friendship with me.

Since arriving in America, I had kept in touch with Hannah, my travelling companion from Sweden. She had moved on to Chicago to be with family, but we exchanged the occasional letter, and Christmas cards. A letter had arrived inviting me to her wedding in six weeks' time. I gratefully accepted. I was able to get some leave, and six weeks later I was on the train to Chicago for a five-day visit.

Chapter Twenty-three

So Conflicted

Having spoken with Betty and Mary, I felt a freedom I had not felt for a long time. I was still not ready for total revelations, but I felt lighter in my being. Also, my visit with Hannah had refreshed me.

I had not seen Michael since our words in the car and in many ways I was sorry for that. Despite everything, I liked him. As far as I was aware he was still involved with Eliza, and his work with the BOI. Deep down, I hoped I would see him again, as I was unhappy our association had ended on a sour note.

A letter came from Sweden full of general news, but between the lines, I was asked how preparations were going for the move of my parents to Vanersborg. I wasn't able to send back much information, as I had not visited Cambridge, or indeed seen my mother for several months. All that I did know was that plans were progressing on schedule.

I still had not made my mind up as to whether to leave America. I rather liked my life and felt I was comfortable making my own decisions, and life certainly had more to offer. I knew too that I liked Jake, but also knew that

I must not build my life around him, and that I must settle things for myself. How things had changed from the rather naive young woman who had first arrived in America, almost five years before, and whose sole quest was to find her parents.

The parents I had found, but it was not quite the reunion I had imagined. I suppose that life generally had intervened, especially living through the war, and more especially spending time with Aunty K, who had become my surrogate mother, sister, aunt and friend. The situation was now reversed and it was Aunty K who was away. I was very troubled, faced with the various choices I could and would have to make.

My work was a welcome relief. I enjoyed my new role as supervisor, particularly the buyer elements of it. I loved being with the customers, in particular the shy young men wanting to buy beautiful trinkets for their beloveds. The New York weather did not bother me, even the heavy snow earlier in the year. Russian winters had been much more severe so, in a strange way, they reminded me of my true home and my life before there was any thought of my quest. Most of all, I enjoyed being part of a group of friends, a sense of belonging, which I loved.

It was soon to be Thanksgiving again and planning had already started for the big parade, which was now to be a yearly event.

Jake appeared. The team had been playing away games. They were still missing their star player, Babe Ruth, and had sadly slipped down in the ratings, but Jake was having the season of his life. I was in many ways surprised to see him, but he seemed happy to see me. I caught Betty's eye and blushed. He looked a little uncomfortable and I thought suddenly he had come to say goodbye. Then he smiled and asked if I would like to walk out again with him on Sunday. This time it was to be Prospect Park. This was a place I knew well, having been ice-skating on the lake, and also Mary and Robert's wonderful wedding had been there. "Yes," I said, "I would like that very much." The time of the meet settled, he wandered off in the direction of the sportswear department, now William's domain. I was relieved; I was not ready to lose another friend. I, for a moment, thought about Michael. My feelings for Jake were different, there was an air of excitement and my heart certainly beat faster whenever he was around. I caught hold of myself and in my sternest, though silent, words, told myself not to read too much into anything. Jake was new to the city, and at present knew few people. This would change, things would go at their own pace, I of all people, knew this.

Sunday came and we went for our stroll around the park, talking and laughing in the same easy manner as the previous time. He asked me questions about my life, and I answered as honestly as I could. A time for revelations may come, but it was not yet.

A few people looked our way, and a couple of the young men, out with their sweethearts, pointed, then whispered to their girlfriends. The further we walked around the park, the more of a stir Jake was causing. I felt nervous, but in his soft voice he said, "Don't worry, you just have to learn to ignore such things. There is no harm meant, I expect they are baseball fans." I smiled and relaxed, that I could relate to, knowing how excited Vivien became every time he came in the store.

After that Sunday we went on a number of walks, attracting more and more attention. He asked me if I would like to go out one evening, to one of the many speakeasy clubs that had sprung up around Manhattan. I said yes, but asked if we could make up a party with my friends, most of whom he had already met. He agreed. I talked to the others the next day, who thought it was a wonderful idea. The two young ones were especially excited, and all agreed to come. William had a friend staying with him, who would also come. They had met at college, before the friend, Oliver, had moved to Philadelphia where most of his family resided. His father was a lawyer, and this was ultimately what Oliver had become. The Davenports were an old, established Pennsylvania family. He and William had met over their shared love of tennis. William also had a new friend, a certain young lady, Lily Craven, whom he had also met through tennis, but this time at the club where he regularly played. She did not join us on this occasion, but we were to meet her many times later.

My friends' lives intrigued me – the various people they knew – and I wondered why William, with his college background, would work in the store. The simple answer was that he liked it; he had his own department, the money and hours suited him, he could continue his hobbies, and he was able to meet new people each day. I could understand that, as it mirrored my own feelings.

Mary and Robert had agreed to come too. Our little gang had had a number of nights out since our big night out when we went to the Cinderella Club to see Bix Biederbecke. However, they had been low-key events and this one promised to be much more. Arrangements made, it was a matter of waiting for it to happen.

Jake and I had talked about various venues around the city, including the Harlem Supper Club. A very popular venue, originally run by the boxer, Jack Johnson, then taken over by Owney Madden, who, rumour had it, was an ex-mobster. It was predominately staffed by African American workers and musicians, and later became the very famous Cotton Club. It was situated within the Harlem section of the city, where much of the housing and facilities had been bought up by Philip A Payton and his Afro-American Realty Company.

I felt that it was better for Jake to visit there with his baseball friends, however I would very much like to visit Carnegie Hall at some point – Andrew Carnegie's famous building, a music venue of great repute. In fact, I had learnt that my countryman, Tchaikovsky, had conducted there on the opening night in 1891, and earlier in the year of 1924, Roland Hayes had given a full length recital, to great acclaim.

There was so much choice, but we opted for a more low-key place on this occasion, as prohibition was still in force so, wherever we went, it carried with it a degree of forbidden excitement. As if my time with Jake wasn't exciting enough. I loved it.

Chapter Twenty-four

Burglary

News came from Cambridge. The student who had been asking all of the questions had been asking more, especially as to when my father had started at the university, and from where. He had been to the records department several times and to the library. The librarian had alerted my mother.

Father had already given notice of leaving and was in the process of packing everything up; a daunting task as there was the house and office items to sort out. Somewhere in the midst of all the chaos, it was noticed that things in the office had been moved, and paperwork rifled through. Alarm bells began to ring with my father. Not long afterwards, there was a burglary at the house. Father suspected that whoever was behind this must be looking for the blueprints and papers, as nothing actually appeared to be missing. It was all very disturbing. The papers in question were not kept in either location, but had sat in a bank strongbox for two decades, coming out on very rare occasions for Father to secretly work on. These occurrences made my parents all the more determined to leave. Their safe haven was safe no longer.

A shipping container had been hired, and all goods going with them were due to be packed therein.

Carl Gustav had offered my father work at his hydroelectric company. This was the reason for leaving, given to the university, but there had been no mention of his relationship to Carl or, more importantly, to Aunty K.

Following the burglaries, the student had disappeared, but my parents still felt very much on edge. I felt sorry I could not be of more comfort to them, but it was decided that all family contact should only be in an emergency. The winter months passed very slowly for us all, and after Christmas, the final items were to be packed, sold or given away. I still felt responsible for this situation, but Aunty K said that she believed that it was fate, and that some good things had come from it. At the very least, the family had been able to join together. In mid-January, of what was now 1926, they moved into a hotel in Boston, and two weeks later to one in New York, to await passage to Gothenburg on the Swedish American Line. All that was left was what to do with the papers and blueprints. A very difficult decision.

My mother was very upset about the whole process and had not really wanted to leave Boston or America but had seen the wisdom of it. Although supportive of Father, she could not help him in his decision. Whichever way it turned out he would be seen as a traitor to one side or the other, a position he found extremely uncomfortable. When this had all first happened he was a young man, full of ideals, with no knowledge of how things would turn out in the future. There had been no war, and man's inhumanity to man had not been shown so vividly. The blueprints, in their pure form, could be used for so much good, but could either side be trusted? Sadly, it was doubtful.

Christmas came and went. Jake had gone back to North Carolina to see his people, and I spent time with Betty's family as I had on previous years. I did manage a carefully planned visit to see my parents once they arrived in New York.

Prior to that, I spent time with Jake, and our night to the speakeasy was great fun and enjoyed by all. We went to several places, causing a stir wherever we went. As we came out of one of the clubs, there were some members of the press, and suddenly there were bulbs popping everywhere. Jake tried to protect me but to no avail; the next day our pictures were in *The Herald*. Jake came to the store and told me not to worry; he had not passed on any information about me, not that he really knew anything anyway. There was a lot of speculation as to who I was. The BOI people were the only ones with any idea, and I didn't suppose they would want my association with them known. However, I waited for my next summons.

It came, as I knew it would. One evening, there was a knock on the door, and there stood Michael in the hallway. "Would you accompany me please, Anna," he said. On the way down to the car, I asked how he was and said I was sorry I was angry the last time we met. He nodded, but didn't answer, although I thought that his body stance softened.

The building was, as usual, busy for the time of day. Again I was taken up to the office of the sinister little man. "What is happening?" I asked. There was no reply, but I sensed the hint of a smile. It put me on edge.

The meeting had a much more formal feel about it and I was immediately asked what my connection was with Vincent Edevanino. *Who?* I stared blankly at the man and said, "I don't know anyone of that name." He again asked me if I knew him. I said vehemently that I did not. Who was he anyway? Apparently he was a bootlegger, connected to one of the New York criminal families, supplying illicit alcohol to the speakeasy clubs I had just started to frequent with Jake. I was shocked and said I knew of no such person. They asked me who I was with on my outings. I was reluctant to say as, strictly, these places were illegal but, as there were so many of them, the police seemed to turn a blind eye. I said that they already knew who I was with as my picture had been in the paper. They smiled at each other knowingly.

"And how do you know him?" one asked.

I answered honestly and said, "Through my workplace."

I thought that was all the questions when suddenly the little man again asked me who I knew in Boston. It completely took me by surprise so, doing my very best to calm myself, I said I didn't know anyone in Boston. They all exchanged glances. I continued by saying the only connection I had was very tenuous. Uncle Carl was an engineer from Sweden who had been to visit a professor at the Massachusetts university. Apparently an expert in his field, Carl had put forward an offer of employment. All to do with engineering or mechanics or some such thing, I wasn't sure. I hoped my answer was vague enough to suffice. I told them that Carl had been on an advisory team in Colorado on some project that was secret and not talked about, and he had decided to visit the professor before he returned home. I said nothing about family connections.

They nodded, muttered amongst themselves, then said I could go. Michael took me to the carpool. He asked me about Jake and I told him honestly that we were friends and enjoyed each other's company. I thought I saw a hint of sadness in his eyes. Whatever might have been was behind us now. A pity as I liked him, and was glad we had been able to speak again. The rest of the journey home was in silence.

Chapter Twenty-five

Shipmates

In early March, Carl Gustav and Aunty K returned to New York. He was again to travel to Colorado for a two-week meeting. Aunty K would be staying at the hotel, as would my parents. This would allow them to meet up under more normal circumstances and hopefully not arouse any suspicions.

My parents had settled all of their affairs and would be travelling to Sweden on the same ship as Aunty K and Carl. I would not be going at this stage as I felt I wanted to stay in New York for a while longer. The blueprints had been removed from the bank in Boston and installed in a local bank. The manager of the bank, Olander Varn, had been affiliated with Carl's family in the distant past, and once family ties had been re-established, he was happy to help. He, of course, was not told the true content of the papers. The decision had been made to take them to Sweden where Father could continue to work on them and change them to be of humanitarian use.

I would go to the hotel after my shift to see Aunty K and, in the process, be 'introduced' to a couple she had met who were coincidentally travelling on the same ship.

It was so good for us all to be together and I think I got to know my mother more than at any other time. Now that she knew she was actually leaving, and felt safer, she became more like the Natasha of old. This was a side of her that I had never seen, but in the company of her sister, the heavy years fell away, and she had a lightness about her. It was hard for me to see a family likeness as the strain had taken its toll, but there was a renewed brightness in her eyes. Father kept pretty much to their rooms, I suppose tying up the loose ends and planning for the future. I doubted he would ever become Sergei again, he seemed to be weighed down with problems.

There were telephones in the lobby, so Aunty K was able to keep in touch with Uncle Carl. The women decided to go on a shopping trip. Firstly they would come to Macy's where, in my lunchbreak, I could show them around, and also reintroduce Aunty K and her new acquaintance to my friends. Aunty K had been to Mary's wedding so had previously met everyone. Some of them had seen her 'friend' very briefly in Central Park with me. However, it was very unlikely that they would remember this person, who looked so different from the dowdy, careworn creature they had seen. I looked more like my father so I hoped no one would make the connection.

The visit to the jewellery department coincided with a visit from Jake, so I was able to introduce him to Aunty K and my mother. He was charming as ever, and I could see the looks of approval in both sets of eyes as he walked away. I smiled sweetly and said I would explain all that evening.

Mary was the only one who showed any sign of recognition, but I quickly took her by the arm and walked in front of the ladies. Mother had a pronounced American accent, and Aunty K's speech, though in English, had a decided Swedish tone to it. Hoping to allay any suspicions, I chatted with Mary and asked how her weekend had been. She and Robert had been to stay with her parents, the Roskell family, in Jersey where her father, Edward, and mother, Isabella, lived. Her father owned a construction firm and had worked on various buildings in Manhattan including the new Cunard Building. She often spoke of her parents, and I had been envious of her relationship with them.

She smiled at us all and returned to her section. I was sure she would have questions later, and once my parents were safely out of the country I could at last be more honest with her. I was so very tired of all of the half-truths and longed to be free of it all. If the truth did come out, I was certain that my father would be forced to work for the military, and it was because of that very reason he had to flee from Russia all those years before.

The two ladies went off to the clothing department, and I returned to my counter. We had a very busy afternoon what with the customers and teaching our new assistant how things worked.

Later, I went to the hotel. On arrival, I was shocked to see Michael in the lobby and quickly moved behind a pillar, hopefully before he saw me. As I watched, a woman came down the stairs and crossed over to him.

It was Eliza, and as they walked by I could hear them discussing going to one of the new restaurants before she was due to perform at the Roseland Ballroom.

I made my way up to the suite and avidly listened while the two sisters told me of the rest of their shopping trip. Each had bought a new outfit and some casual clothes, mainly for taking part in the ship's many onboard activities. They had also been to some of the other stores on 5th Avenue, thoroughly enjoying their time together. I was happy for them; this time had been many years in the making. Sweden was going to seem very different from the bustle of New York City. Father had gone down to the smoking room to enjoy a whisky and a cigar.

After a couple of hours, it was time for me to return home. Father had still not returned to the suite, so I said I would look for him on the way out. I crossed the foyer en route to the smoking room and, to my horror, at the bar I could see father talking to Michael. I had thought he was with Eliza, but here he was talking to the professor. I decided it was best to walk on but Michael saw me and beckoned me over to say hello. I was in a state of panic. My resemblance, close up, to my father was much more apparent, and how would I explain that, if asked? I waved from where I stood and gestured that I had to leave as it was getting late. Outside I hurried away on my homeward journey.

The following evening I went to the hotel with Jake, who said he would accompany me to see Aunty K, whom he had met and liked. I was grateful for his support. Up in the suite, I left him with Aunty K and her new 'friend' whilst I went to find Father. He was in a buoyant mood, so carefully I asked him if he knew who he had been speaking with in the bar. He was unaware, so I reminded him who Michael was and of my relationship with him and the BOI. I told him about the evening visits and the fact that they had never made it clear why I was there. They talked mainly about my papers, and Hannah, the young lady I had travelled with from Sweden, whose people were from Chicago. I said that perhaps they thought she had criminal links as I had also been asked about a certain known supplier of illicit alcohol. Were these just smoke screens? I didn't really know. I also told him that, on my last visit, they had asked me if I knew anyone from Boston. I, of course, had said no.

Father took my hand, and in the gentle voice that I remembered from early childhood, told me not to worry. His discussion with Michael had been very general, mainly about New York life and baseball. I felt a little relieved, but also begged him to be on his guard as I knew how the members of the BOI went about their business, asking innocuous questions. They were so close to leaving America; it would be a tragedy if things went wrong at this late stage.

There were, as far as I knew, no more meetings so perhaps it was just coincidence, as Father had said. Carl came back from Colorado having finished the project, which would later become known as the Boulder Dam.

They finalised their plans, their ship due to leave in three days.

Chapter Twenty-six

Warnings

Michael appeared one late afternoon at the end of my shift, waiting outside the store. He waved and beckoned to me. My heart sank; he had never come to the store before. Was I to be arrested? I wandered over to him.

"I have come to warn you," he said, "someone from Boston has filed a report against someone known to you, or at least to Carl Gustav."

I stared at him, and hoped he could not hear the loud beating of my heart. "A report?" I managed to say. "Regarding what?"

"Walk with me," he said.

As we walked away from the store, I was in a state of turmoil. What could have happened? I stopped and turned to him and said, "I really don't understand what this is all about, not now or in the past. All of the questions at your office have really unnerved me. I came to America to start a new life where I was told there were many opportunities, and I have been treated like a criminal."

His expression softened and he said, "For that I am sorry. There was a problem with your papers and the fact that your life only seemed to have started in your teenage years. Where was the early part of your life spent?"

Mustering all of my courage, I replied, "In Sweden, as I have told you."

I could see that he didn't really believe me. "Anna, I have come to care about your welfare, and that is why I am here now." I relaxed a little, but was still very much on my guard. "I believe," he went on, "that your uncle, Carl Gustav, has been in touch with a certain professor from Massachusetts University, and it is in regard to this man that a complaint has been made."

I steadied my breathing and replied in the calmest way I could, "It was about a job in engineering, back in Sweden, I believe." I reminded him that Carl had been a guest of the government, brought to America as an expert advisor for some, as yet, secret project in Colorado, the details of which I was not privy to, and had not been discussed by Uncle Carl. He nodded because, of course, he already knew that. Nonchalantly I asked him, what sort of complaint.

"I cannot give you any details, except to say he is under investigation regarding nationality issues."

I was indignant, and said, "Well, he is Swedish, his family are from Vannersborg."

Michael smiled that strange enigmatic smile of his and said softly, "No, Anna, not Carl Gustav, the professor."

"Oh," I said, "as far as I am aware, he is an American. Carl had read of his work, and endeavoured to meet him whilst in America."

He smiled again and said, "I just wanted to tell you that they are all in danger of arrest. Also," he added, "I will deny that this conversation took place."

I nodded and our conversation turned to more mundane matters. I asked how life was treating him, and if he was still walking out with the young lady I had seen him with. "You mean Eliza? Oh yes, for some while now."

"I wish you happiness," I said, and thanked him for his concern for me.

He walked me to the nearest subway station, and I rode the train home. Staring out of the train windows I thought about how different it might have been if he had not been in the BOI, but then I wouldn't have met him. Besides which, I had now met Jake.

Once in my apartment, I made myself my usual comfort drink that always soothed me in times of upset. I needed to get a message to Aunty K but felt that I must not leave the apartment block in case I was followed. On the ground floor lived Stanley, the self-appointed caretaker of the building. I had spoken to him on rare occasions, and I knew he had a telephone. I went to him and explained there was a family crisis and that I needed to phone the hotel where other relatives were staying to let them know. He reluctantly agreed. I phoned the reception area and asked to be put through to Aunty K's room. After what seemed an age, the phone was picked up. In Swedish I asked who I was talking to and, to my relief, it was Aunty K. I told her I was using the phone in my apartment block and must be quick. I told her of Michael's visit and that I wasn't really sure if it was from concern, or was the laying of a trap, and that was why I hadn't come to the hotel. She said she would talk with Carl and get my parents moved elsewhere until the boat was due to sail, in two days' time. I said that I didn't think I would be able to visit there again, but perhaps she could come to the store to say goodbye. Stanley was becoming agitated, so I replaced the receiver and burst into tears.

Stanley looked at me and said, "I didn't know you were foreign."

Through my snuffles, I said indignantly, "I'm not, I'm American, but these relatives were from Sweden, a language taught to all family members as children." He seemed satisfied with the explanation. I went back to my apartment and had a very restless night.

Work at the store went very slowly and I expected to be taken away for questioning at any moment. Betty was concerned for me, but I used my usual excuse of having a restless night, upset that Aunty K would be leaving again for Sweden. Our new assistant, Vivien, busied herself restocking the counters. It reminded me of when I first worked at the store, rearranging the displays.

In fact, it was during one of my trips to sort out new stock that I had found the newspaper fragment that had sent me on my way to Cambridge and the eventual location of my parents.

Aunty K came alone to the store the next day. During my break, she was able to tell me that my parents had moved to another hotel, near to the pier from where the ship was sailing. They, and this included Aunty K and Uncle Carl, were travelling to Gothenburg on the MS *Gripsholm*, the first diesel-powered motor vessel, just commissioned this year, 1926. Carl Gustav had booked all of the tickets, and my parents were travelling under their Swedish identities. Just one more day, and hopefully everyone would be safe.

The student who had been asking questions had been sent by, we believed, the Soviet government under an assumed identity to find out about my father, and, like me, had followed a trail starting from Irkutsk. As the blueprints had never surfaced, it had been assumed that either they had been totally destroyed, or that, as was really the case, were being kept safely somewhere. It had been an old case, brought again to the fore when the new government had taken power. Once the search had been narrowed down to America, Stalin and his cronies could not risk that the papers would fall into American hands. We – that is, Aunty K, Uncle Carl and my parents – were just pawns in this lethal game of chess.

The day of the sailing arrived and I stayed at work – just another day for me to any prying eyes. It saddened me greatly not to say goodbye, but I knew in my heart it would not be the last time I would see my parents.

Throughout the day I knew I was being watched, and although my direct connection was not known, I was under investigation. Aunty K and Uncle Carl had stayed away from my parents and they would not have contact with each other until the ship had safely left American waters. Carl had secured new papers for my parents; his wealth opening many doors. They were now a couple by the names of Anna-Marie and Petter Johansson, returning home after visiting relatives in Utica, upstate New York. Father had darkened his now greying hair, and Mother no longer looked like the dull secretary of the American professor.

My parents boarded first, with no problems, using their new papers and were shown to their cabin in the second class area. Aunty K and Carl, as befitted their status, had a suite in first class. Once at sea, they could strike up a friendship and spend time together. I learnt of the leaving of the ship from *The Herald*, complete with pictures as the new vessel sailed out of the harbour. All other information I learned later in a coded letter from Aunty K.

The following day, Michael came to the store and, from a distance, acknowledged me. It seemed we both knew what had taken place, and I was grateful for his discretion, if not just a little perplexed as to why. I would see him from time to time with Eliza when she was performing at various clubs. My friendship with Jake had deepened, and yet I think we both knew I was not the one for him. His glamorous lifestyle, the constant hassle by the press and the fact that he was away for much of the season put a strain on our relationship. However, we were able to remain as friends, which we both cherished.

In 1928, I decided it was time to leave and return to Sweden. I told my friends that I wished to spend more time with Aunty K and Uncle Carl, and longed for a simpler life. They were the only family I had really known. I made my peace with Michael, although he still didn't know the whole truth. I had had the most amazing time with Jake, and he was becoming the star player that he had always promised to be.

My friends were sad, as was I. Eight years had passed and with them many changes. We had all had fun, and each one of us had settled into a different life. Robert had left the store and taken his place in his father's empire, with Mary at his side. They now had a daughter, whom they called Anna. I was honoured. The girls – well, young women now – still enjoyed life to the full, and William had met the love of his life, Lily. I was still alone, but not unhappy – who knew what Sweden would have to offer.

Before I left, I talked to Mary and told her some of the details of my life, knowing that she would hold my secrets in her heart. I didn't want to burden her so I was still selective in what I told her, but I wanted to be as honest as I could with her as she was very intuitive, and always had my welfare at heart. Even though we were close in age, I thought of her as my American Aunty K.

By coincidence, the ship I booked passage on was the now MS *Drottningholm*, newly refurbished and back in service on the New York-Gothenburg line. It made me smile as I boarded, as it was on this very ship I had arrived with Hannah, years earlier, excited to start my new life in America.

The circle forever turns.

Chapter Twenty-seven

Circle complete

It was hard to believe how quickly time had gone by, and how many things had happened.

I was happy, settled with one child – a boy named Stephan – and another child expected in the coming months. Aunty K and Uncle Carl were in a loving relationship, comfortable in their way of life. He had been asked back to America now that work was due to commence on the construction of the dam in Colorado, where he had originally taken part as an advisor in the planning stages. Aunty K would, in any event, stay in Sweden, running the estate. Carl, knowing her love of horses, had built up a stable of the finest thoroughbreds, of which she was in charge.

My mother and father had fitted into Swedish country life very easily, reminding them, I think, of their younger days growing up around Lake Baikal. This was, of course, before life took its toll on everyone. Carl had provided working space for my father to continue his research using the blueprints. I did not really understand what it was all about as it was all kept very secret. What little I did know was that it involved large metal structures. The result, I was to learn many years later, was to create light, in the form of a powerful beam, to be used as a power source. A cheap source of energy for all. However, sadly, this kind of invention could also be used as a weapon, if adapted, and this was why my father had taken the plans so many years before. Working with Carl in his facilities would be of some guarantee of the power being used for purposes of good.

We had all heard of the dreadful 1929 Wall Street Crash, and of how it had affected many families, including those of my friends. Mary and Robert's families seemed particularly affected. I felt such sorrow for them. William seemed to have escaped the worst of it, and the two girls, now also married, seemed to have weathered that particular storm. There were so many changes to everyone's lives, directly affected or not.

As the new decade had dawned it didn't seem possible for such turmoil and changes, but life and circumstances never stay still, and this decade was to be no different.

And what of me? Well, I too had left America, having spent an amazing eight years there. What times I had had, so many experiences, enriched by the wonderful people I had met. I loved my little apartment, my safe haven. I enjoyed working at the store with Emily, Betty and Vivien, and all the customers I had the pleasure to serve and become part of their lives for a few moments. Best of all, I loved spending time with my very special friends, who looked after me, treated me well and made me a part of their group when I was a stranger and alone. I was especially fond of Mary and was deeply honoured when she called her daughter Anna, after me. Even though that was not my real name, it was to my American friends. Before I had left, I told her more of my life, and in her kind and understanding way said she could understand how important it had been to find my family. A beautiful girl with a beautiful nature. We had both cried as our emotions overwhelmed us.

I had also spent many happy hours with Jake, but as his fame grew I knew that lifestyle was not for me. I had experienced a touch of the glamorous life, and that was enough for me. He said he understood and valued my friendship above all else, and so we parted on good terms. I was to hear of his marriage, some years later, to a very stunning New York socialite from one of the old established families; a Miss Elizabeta von Scharfe. I was happy for him. Mary and I kept in touch and her letters were always full of news and a pleasure to read.

So, who did I marry? Well, it was my first real love, Hans. I returned to Sweden to find him working for Carl Gustav. His first wife had sadly died in childbirth, after which he had moved to Sweden on Aunty K's recommendation. He had brought his daughter with him. A beautiful blond child named Marta, who I loved as my own. So, like Carl, he was able to find happiness a second time around.

Everything had come almost full circle, and although we were not back in Russia, we were back together as a family. I was getting to know my parents much more, and they revelled in their roles as grandparents. I had wondered through the years if I had done the right thing in searching for them, but when I saw everyone together again I knew it had been the right thing to do. Besides which, my beloved Aunty K had assured me that the family gatherings would never have happened without our search.

Sadly, many years earlier, Aunty Aninya had died, so all that was left was to get Aunty Elena and Mikhail out of Russia, and back into the fold, and then the rejoining of all of the broken pieces would be complete.

Another quest perhaps?

List of Characters and Locations

A

Anna/Anastasia/Algebra
Aunty A (Aninya)
Aunty E (Elena)
Aunty K (Katya)
Alice
Astor Hotel
America

B

Bureau of Investigation (BOI)
Boulder Dam
Bix Biederbecke
Babe Ruth
Betty (Store)
Boston Red Sox
Blizzard
Bridesmaids

C

Carl Gustav
Cinderella Club
Central Park
Cambridge
Colorado
Cotton Club

D
Dam - America, Sweden
Duke Ellington

E
Emily (Store)
Eliza Worthington
Elizabeta von Scharfe

F
Fletcher Henderson Orchestra
Floats
Frederik Olaf
Frieda

G
Games - Tennis, Baseball
Gothenburg
Gallagher Michael

H
Haven
Hotel - Astor
Hans

I
Ice and Snow

J
Jacob (Jake) Carruthers
Jewellery Department

K
Kris Kringle

L
Lizzie
Lake
Lenin
Lily Craven

M
Mary
Michael (BOI)
Macy's Store
Mikhail
Massachusetts
Marta

N
New York
Natasha
Nursery Rhymes

O
Oliden Hydroelectric Plant
Oliver Davenport
Olander Varn

P
Prospect Park Boathouse

Q
Questions

R
Robert
Roseland Ballroom
Roskell Edward and Isabella

S
Santa Claus
Sergei
Sinister little man
Stalin
Sjonsson
Stephan
Ships – MS *Gripsholm,* MS *Drottningholm*
Sweden

T
Thanksgiving Parade
Tom Turkey

U
Uncle Carl
Uncle Mikhail
USSR

V
Vincent Edevanino
Vivien Hughes

W
William
Wedding

X
Xander Berksley

Y
Yankees – Stadium, baseball team

Z
Zen place

Locations

New York City, New York, USA
Buffalo, New York, USA
Utica, New York, USA

Jersey City, Jersey, USA

Boston, Massachusetts, USA
Cambridge, Massachusetts, USA

Chicago, Illinois, USA

Colorado, USA

Pennsylvania, USA

North Carolina, USA

Brasov, Romania
Suceavea, Romania

Gothenburg, Sweden
Vannersborg, Sweden

Lake Baikal, Siberia, Russia
Irkutsk, Russia
Moscow, Russia

Acknowledgements

My thanks to Simon Hadfield and Penny Knight for their support in everything.

To Lez Harvey for the cover design.

To Chris Hadfield and Steph Summers for the reworking of all photographs/drawings, and technical know-how.

To Christine Emery, Jean Olsson-Law and David Law for lending me their ears.

To Karen Crick, Jen Wilson and Sandra Gardner for listening to all of my story updates, and for all of their input.

To Gill Langley for helping with the research during our weekly telephone chats.

To Natalie, Collette, Adrienne, Vicky, Jo and everyone who encouraged me in my scribblings and ramblings.

To my three cats, Ellie-May, Mali-Blue and Devon Lacey who waited patiently for their food and cuddles.

To Dean, Becky, Tania, Julie, and all staff at Grosvenor House Publishing Ltd. for their support, advice and encouragement.

Research

To Wikipedia, City Archives, Boulder Dam and information on New York life in the 1920s.

Information regarding Babe Ruth and the New York Yankees.

Information on Bix Biederbeck, various Orchestras and Ballrooms, and the Bureau of Investigation (BOI) of 1924/25.

Photographic archives of Macy's Department Store.

Thanksgiving Parade (1924), various events and notable buildings in New York and the surrounding areas in the 1920s.

'Algebra', from the Arabic al-jabr word meaning the 'reunion of broken parts'.